All persons in this story are entirely fictitious and bear no resemblance to anyone I have met.

Most of the locations are real and they are some of my favourite places.

Novels by Adrienne Nash

Trudi; ~ Trudi in Paris; ~ Trudi and Simon; ~ Trudi without Simon.

Breakdown.

Long Journey into Light.

Castle Murkie.

The Trials of Sienna Chambers.

The Cellar; ~ and sequel, ~ A Time to be Brave.

Elizabeth.

A Strange Life (Autobiography of the Author)

Tina G.

To Love and Love Not.

Coming Out.

From the Ashes.

From the Ashes

By
Adrienne Nash

Chapter 1.   Nick's Tale

In the beginning there was just me, not that I remember that time. No one remembers much before their third birthday and by the time I had that cake with the three candles, he was only a couple of months. He, Ed spent most of the time crying. I was supposed to be thrilled to have this wailing infant in the house. Mum and Dad had made a great thing of telling me I was getting a brother, someone to play with, but when it arrived, I found it was too precious for me to touch.

By the time my four-candle cake arrived, it, Edward as I now managed to call him had calmed down. He actually began to play and be a nuisance. If I was playing with anything, he would want it. Usually he picked it up and tried to bite it, but having no proper teeth, he would just dribble over it and then I would shout at him and mum would come and tell me not to shout and say, 'Go and wash your brick or whatever. Remember Edward's only a baby. Be nice.'

I started school about then, well I had play school first and that was OK, at least I was away from the brat. School was good because we were taught sports and I really liked that. We played footie in the winter and in break time too, kicking a ball around the playground. I was good at it and dad, when he was home played with me. He took me to the park and taught me ball control, like when it was passed to me, stopping it with a soft foot so it didn't immediately bounce off a few yards. I think dad had been quite a good footballer when he was young.

In the summer we played cricket and I soon got the hang of that. The trick as dad explained was to watch that ball from the time the bowler's leg passed the wicket. Lot's of people just focus on the ball where they expect it to bounce. Fatal. Dad explained it all, that you had to see the bowlers arm passing his shoulder and the ball coming from there. You could understand a lot about what sort of ball to expect by watching. It was all split second stuff. The wicket crease to crease is only twenty metres and if that ball is coming at even forty miles an hour, it's not easy to adjust. Dad said reaction had to be instinctive. We played cricket a lot in the garden. He mowed a patch of lawn so it was like a real wicket and he bowled at me, slow and fast, spin and swing. Once you get your eye in, you can hit anything. From somewhere he actually got nets so the ball didn't rocket through the flowers mum planted or his pride and joy, runner beans and rhubarb.

When he was home and we had the time, we went to the rec, the recreation ground, a public sports field and we would get whoever to play with us. Dad usually ended up being the umpire. He also thought he was Arsene Wenger, the Arsenal FC football manager. He worshipped that team and it grieved him that at times, they were, well rubbish, passing the ball about as if frightened to bang it at the goal. He used to swear at the TV and that used to bring a sharp telling off from mum to watch his language. I used to think, well I've heard worse than that in the playground and used it, so what's the fuss mum. I mean the F word and bloody and bugger. So when dad swore at the TV, I just grinned. Sometimes I do say fuck, like when I fell off my bike into a tree on the track in the woods.

It, my little brother, Edward isn't interested in sport at all. When I was five and kicking a ball quite well, he couldn't do it at all at that age. Cos by then I was nearly eight, and captain of the primary school team. Even when I was ten, he was nearly eight, he was still rubbish, kicked like a girl, and it was annoying because the idea was to pass it between us and it would go anywhere, which meant I was having to go fetch from next door or even in the street. When I said he was useless he would get mad and pick the ball up and throw it over the fence into next door, then he would clear off to see his friend Jenny. He knew he was safe from a clobbering there.

By the time I'd gone next door and retrieved my ball, I'd cooled down. He was a poor kid, not much good as a brother. He could read at four, me, I was seven and then I only wanted to read about sport. Mum keeps on that I should try harder because even if I make it to play for Arsenal, I might get crocked and have a short career before I make a fortune. Dad says, 'well look at me, I've done OK. I make good money.'

'Yes,' she says, 'risking your life in a diving bell in the North Sea, apart from the helicopter flights. How long before something goes wrong and, they won't employ you as a diver after forty.'

Then there's a bit of domestic and grandma features quite a bit and then sometimes Edward, how good he is at school and dad says, more like a bloody girl than a boy. That does it. Bloody girl. Mum says don't you swear about women. Dad says Ed's not female. And mum says, 'you said bloody girl and he says I didn't mean it like that,' and then she says, 'why did you say it then? Football and sport are not the only things worth doing in this world. He's already reading things you wouldn't understand.'

Dad will then go quiet. But mum, she can dredge up things from ages ago, it's like he's thrown a brick and she throws back a cart load of bricks and he sits as if dodging them, shifting in his seat. Then he says I'm going out.

He'll disappear for a couple of hours down the pub or he bungs his clubs in the car and off to golf for six hours, playing with whoever. He plays off twelve. That's pretty damn good considering he's on a rig for a lot of the time.

These days, I don't see much of Ed. He's always got his head in a book and now he has a laptop he's into that. I just look at the sport on mine and play a few games. He does all sorts and if there's ever a problem with the computer, he can sort it. I don't know how. The rest of the time he's with Jenny Jennings. They live at the bottom or top of our garden. Our garden being on a corner plot, runs up parallel to the side street and The Jenning's is number one in that street Whenever Ed is upset or mum and dad row, he's off up there and I've seen him playing all sorts of girlie games. Hopscotch, skipping, pretend tea parties. Had a spell when he wouldn't even talk to me, us, after mum asked when he and Jenn were getting married. He was mad as hell. He stormed off to his room and I caught him lying on the bed, cuddled up with that bear and crying. I don't get him at all. He's a rum boy.

He didn't know I saw. I peeped through the crack between hinge and door surround. I told mum. 'He has to harden up,' she said, but I could see she's worried.

I've tried to be more kind since then. Most of the time I leave him alone. Sometimes he gets bullied at school because he's always with the girls and I have to look after him there. I punched Jimmy Richards on the nose, taught him a lesson to keep his hands off my little brother. Got sent to the head and got off, said I was protecting my blood. Next time he said come to me or another teacher. Yes sir. Like hell, kids don't take any notice and bullying can be so subtle, there's often nothing to see. I good belt usually stops it. I do wish Ed could be more of a boy.

I told mum and she didn't reply, just frowned and sighed. I think that's why she teases him over Jenn, trying to get him to open up. He hardly speaks to us, spends more and more time with the Jennings, even going on holiday with them at Easter. Well I can understand that, Jenn is a good kid, pretty girl too and as an only child she must be lonely. I don't know what goes on in Ed's mind. Like the only time he's alive is with Jenn. Round the house he's so quiet. He helps mum a lot, like shopping, laying the table, cooking. Even dusting. Christ. That really is girl stuff, I mean serious girl stuff. His room is not a boy room. He has ornaments. All set out, like he has a china cat and dog, bought at the jumble, and another of one of those milkmaid statues, girl in a long blue dress and lace under, in china, and sometimes flowers in a vase. If they were in my room they would just stay until they went brown and crisp and the water would go rank and stinking. No, not in his room, he wouldn't let that happen.

When he was at Jenn's I had a good chat with mum. She asked if I'd heard about transgender, transsexual? I said yeah, I knew all about it, seen it on TV, this kid, kids, boys living as girls, even a few girls living as boys. Funny thing was, they looked OK, I mean you couldn't tell. Mum asked if I thought Ed was like that? I dunno. Christ, I said, that would be a bit of a bummer. Rotten. Why would anyone choose to be a girl? Those fancy fussy things they do and cooking and house work. Mum gives me this cross look. That's not what being a girl, a woman is all about she says. Well, I say, defensively, it's some of it. Unfortunately, because men have arranged this bloody world, yes, she says, but it needn't be, and go and tidy your room. Take the hoover I want to see it spotless.

'It's not about me,' I say. 'It's about Ed. Sorry mum. Are you really worried?'

'He's so clever, but he won't speak. I've tried teasing about Jenn and girls' games, asked outright why he likes being with her and girls so much and he just says they're nice. If you watch more of those transgender programmes, you would see it isn't a choice. They have brains that are female, that's why they want to do girl things. He likes doing girl things. Rebecca says it's like having two girls when they're together.'

'Why not just ask him?'

'I'm frightened of pushing him in that direction. It's got to come from him. He has to feel so strongly that he has the confidence to confide in us. He hardly speaks to any of us. Yet Rebecca says, when he's with them, he and Jenn never stop. He is so happy with her. It's almost as though it's all our fault and we've been rejected.'

'His room's girly. He still hugs that teddy bear. He cries a lot.'

'Yes, well a lot of that's you.'

'Well I try to get him to fight back. Instead he gives that killer look he has, almost cross eyed, I mean what d'you call it, like his eyes are looking into your soul.'

'Intense stare. Yes, almost as if he's trying to make sense of the world, not just us. His eyes seem to get darker in colour with that intensity. It's not my imagination then?'

'No mum, we've all had that look.'

'Wonder whether I should take him to a psychiatrist.'

'He might grow out of it. He's not nuts. He's really clever, top in everything, you see his report. The only thing is games, can't do toffee.'

"I looked on his laptop, the history, to see if there was a clue there. No history, well just some harmless ones on films and some history for his homework. The rest was wiped.'

'Should I ask mum? He might tell me, you know kids don't like telling parents everything.'

'You don't ask if he wants to be a girl, I don't want that idea put in his head.'

'OK. I'll just ask what's bugging him. I know what he'll say, you, me I'll be bugging him. He's so clever; he can just run rings round me with his reasoning. I feel like an idiot. I say something mean and his mind just zooms off into overdrive and he destroys me. I come away smarting. Because I can't win the arguments, I feel like bashing him. No, I don't mum. I usually pretend laugh and walk away.'

'I know what you mean. Well, have a go at talking to him, nicely. Look out for him Nicky. Protect him.'

'I do mum but it's hard looking out for someone that seems to hate me.'

Chapter 2.   Nick's Tale

My twelfth birthday. I go to the climbing wall at the sports centre. It's fifty feet on the end gable wall of the swimming pool. OK so it's all on a rope and a harness, but it still takes strength and guts to just hand by a hand and foot by foot, climb that wall. That moment when you fall off, just the first half second dropping, gives a jolt. It's me and six kids from school and of course Ed and if Ed's there, then so is Jenn. She's getting really pretty.

Anyway I'm surprised when Ed gets harnessed up to climb. He doesn't have to, but he said he'd have a go. He's white as a sheet, looks absolutely terrified. He gets up about ten feet and then looks down and says he can't do it and of course the kids jeer. He falls off and he's lowered to the floor. Before they can take the harness off, he starts again. He gets half way and he looks down. I see his little face. He's actually crying. I say to the instructor, 'Bring him down.'

The instructor shakes his head. 'Let him conquer his fear. He can't come to any harm. He's still climbing, still thinking, searching for the next hold. Oh crikey, that was a good move. He wouldn't get away with that if he was heavier, but well done.' He was sort of forty-five degrees across the vertical.

He reached the top and everyone cheered. He dropped off and came to the bottom on the rope. He was still crying but laughing too. He and Jenn embraced and did that jumping up and down thing I hate. So girly. But I was proud of little brother. Mum was proud too.

We went to a burger joint for our tea. Burgers are banned in our household but allowed as a treat. We all had milk shakes as well and ice cream sundaes. It was brilliant.

I told Ed how well he'd done and he just looks at me with that disdainful look as though anything I say is not worth hearing and turns back to Jenn. They are there giggling about something. He really is a girl. I said to mum, 'Had she checked inside his shorts lately, to make sure he has the right bits?'

Mum wasn't impressed.

After that climbing wall thing, I had a different opinion of my bro. He was far more complicated than I thought. He wasn't just a Sissy Boy playing girly games. There's something, seriously wrong with him, I do know that, I mean hardly a boy trait. Clean, sweet smelling. With strangers and relations, he's polite and smiling but with us sullen, almost as if he hates us and the World. Mum spoke to Rebecca. Rebecca can't speak highly enough, loves him she says, as if he were her own, the child she lost.

While mum was pleased, I think she was almost insulted that her kid, who cannot stand us, is so well thought of in Rebecca's household.

I can understand that. It must be like a real slap in the face with a wet fish for mum. Her baby doesn't hardly want anything to do with us, but next door, is loving and outgoing, well mannered and talkative.

It's like when we had people come to tea and we were all eating sandwiches and cakes on our knees, he's carrying the plates around and asking if they'd like more. OK, I spose that's the thing to do, but it was a bit girly with his girly smile.

Dad can't do with baby brother at all. He just shrugs. Sometimes he says, I wish I'd had two boys. 'That's a bit harsh,' I say in a rare moment of adulthood, well I am only twelve.

'Dad he's good at other stuff. I should be more like him.' Meaning of course, doing my homework and such instead of playing street footie and going to the local club for coaching. I ought to have my nose in a book more often.

'One sissy is enough.' He replies.

My thirteenth birthday. Nothing has changed much except the number of candles. This time we go to a theme

Park, not the best but it was OK fun and not too far in the car. The brat, my brother is there and of course Jenn. I'm surprised that bro goes on all the rides. I can see he's frightened but he does it anyway. There are nine of us, six of my friends and me, and bro and Jenn.

Ed hasn't changed. He's ten but just as girly. He flies off the handle easily and the rest of the time doesn't speak to dad or me. He helps mum a lot. He now refuses to have his hair cut. In desperation and exasperation, I asked if he would rather he had been a girl. 'Why?' he asks. I said. 'Well, you're so obviously not a boy.

He put his nose in the air, the way he does, so bloody annoying, and he said, 'You'd know would you?'

What's that mean? Even when I try to be nice, he just treats me as if I'm some sort of idiot. I swear I could thump him at times. With his hair long, he's even prettier, even more like a girl. He's really out of control. Dad can't do anything with him and mum won't. She says she has to let his true character come out, even if he drives us all mad.

I know Mum's right. I also know if he would only trust us with what bothers him, this would be a much happier family and he would be happier too.

Winter term starts and I like it because it's football season again. Arsenal draw two out of three matches. It's a bad start. Anyway back to school and I'm Captain of the colts, even though all the rest are older and in a form above.

Dad is so proud of me and mum has to tell him to cool it when he's at a match and shouting from the side lines, telling all my team mates to pass it to me. It's bloody embarrassing. My mates all poke fun. I shall have to tell him to cool it. Shit that'll be hard, telling my dad off.

This Saturday we're going to the Emirates, Arsenal versus Spurs, North London derby match, the old enemies. It's always great fun, except when people get out of hand. Mostly it's just a lot of shouting, bravado as dad says, all mouth and trousers. It's a draw, one one. It's awful and the fans aren't pleased. There's a few boos and placards against Wenger. Everyone at Arsenal are disappointed while Tottenham feel damned lucky to have come to the Emirates and got a point.

What makes it worse is that we sit at tea glum and little bro laughs. 'It's only a silly game.'

'It's not silly.' I retort, snappily. 'What would a soppy girl like you know anyway?'

He goes red and I see I've hit home. His eyes fill and he stands up to his full four feet five inches. I think he's going to hit me and so I laugh like, it would only be a chicken shit hit anyway. And he does. Fast wham a smack right in the face, not a fist, a girly smack. I see red and stand and mum shouts, 'Stop it both of you. I won't have it.'

Dad says quietly. 'Edward go to your room and stay there.'

'No.'

'Edward, go to your room!' Mum says and he looks at her as though he hates her. Really. I think he's going to refuse then he walks from the kitchen head up and I hear him thumping up the stairs, deliberately loudly. A door slams and after the loo flushes. Then his bedroom door slams. Then I hear a howl. It's not a sound I care to hear. It's like a wolf in the wilderness, but high pitched. It's a sound of utter torment, wretchedness, mum says.

'Now look what you've done between the pair of you. As though that child is not unhappy enough.'

'He started it.'

'He is only nine. Take no notice.'

'Nearly ten,' I say.

'He needs straightening out.' Dad says.

'Oh and you know how do you?" Mum says.

Dad shrugs. It's been a bad enough day with a draw to Tottenham. Now a domestic. I have tea and then I go out in the last of the evening light and practice tricks with the ball, keeping it up, catching it on my back and I'm trying to perfect it rolling up one arm and down the other. I look up and I see a small face in the bedroom window. I feel really bad. I bite my lip. For the first time ever, I feel real love for him and wish that row hadn't happened. It's not like Ed to use violence. He's usually a snotty kid, using his mouth to fight back or annoy.

He's still watching. I look up and salute. I mouth sorry and I see him smile. Goddammit.

Winter term and school football goes pretty well. We win most matches. I also start at another local club, Chelhampton United, playing in the reserves and I get spotted and I get a trial for another East London club, only league two but then I'm only just thirteen. I get a letter five days later. They want to sign me up for their youth team. Mum's not pleased, she says more running about and days tied up, midweek practice and weekends as though she hasn't enough to do when dad's away on the rigs. I do see her point.

She agrees to do her best.

'And what do I do?' Ed asks.

'I'll speak to Rebecca.'

'I might as well live there.' He says.

'You almost do now playing your girly games.' I say.

'Oh so what?'

'Stop it this minute!' mum says.

'Football. Poofball all that kissing.'

'Yeah well, you'd no about poofs.'

'Well there's a lot you don't know, idiot.'

He's hit me where it hurts; I am an idiot, nearly bottom of my class.

Mum steps in again. 'Go and wash your hands and see what Jenn's doing Edward.'

'That's where I was going anyway.'

'Why don't you live there?' I say. 'Your fuck all use to me as a brother.'

'Stop it this minute. I can't do with this and watch your language Nicholas or you can say goodbye to training with your new team.'

'He...' I stop. There's no point and I can see mum's near to tears. 'I'm sorry mum. He winds me up. I'll try to ignore it.'

'You also wind him up. Leave him alone. He doesn't like the same things as you; nothing says he has to like football. He doesn't make you study, though God knows I wish he could. He has a lot of qualities you could do with.'

'Yes mum, I know. I wish I could understand him.'

'You and me and especially your father. If it wasn't for Rebecca and Jenny, I don't know what we'd do. Now promise me, you'll try to ignore his jibes, don't wind him up and turn the other cheek. He's only a kid and Nick, language please.'

'Yes mum.'

I get up and I kiss her. I'm nearly as tall.

Chapter 3.   Nick's Tale

Christmas and dad isn't home. It's just the three of us. More often than not, it's just mum and me. Littl'un leaves us after breakfast and marches up the garden to see Jenn taking her present and one for her dad and mum.

'What did he get her?'

'Some dance clothes. Rebecca bought them and he paid for them and he wrapped them.'

'How long's he going to be up there?'

'Half an hour. Rebecca and I worked it out between us. He'll be back to open presents here, and then we are going up there for drinks and a late Christmas Lunch. They are coming down here for late tea, cold turkey, ham, pickles and salad and Christmas cake, mince pies, trifle. OK?'

'I spose. Can I go out and kick about?'

'First load the dishwasher, properly. Then you can go out and kick about for an hour. You come in and change into your knew chinos and that preppy button down shirt. I want you smart for going up there.'

'Yes mum. Mum,' I kiss her. 'Happy Christmas.'

'Thank you dear. I think I said that an hour ago. But happy Christmas to you. Don't go upsetting the applecart today, no rows, no bullying. Promise me.'

'Ma I'll be good. Don't you know it's Christmas?'

Christmas day went fine. The two girls, I mean Jenn and Ed amused themselves with girly things, and then in the afternoon we three played Monopoly. They wanted to play Scrabble but I'm no good at that.

I'm next to Jenn and I can smell her hair. I want to get closer and I do so by sort of wriggling about and she looks at me sideways. Does she know? Oh God, now I swear I'm blushing.

The game went on too long and then it was Christmas tea and the girls, Jenn, Ed and mum laid out the buffet tea. I think it was better than lunch, lots of cold meats, some pickles, and potato salad with chives and not too much salad. Smashing. I have a sip of Mr Jennings beer too. Actually it's been a nice day. I do my duty, filling the dishwasher while the women put stuff away. It looks like we have enough food for a month, still as mum says, I'm a growing boy and I'll do my bit.

It was soon New Year and a week later dad came home. I'm playing for North Ham Rovers reserves, first Saturday, and I actually score a goal even though we lose one three. Dad chats to the manager and as we drive home in London traffic, dad is full of it. I think he sees himself as my agent, taking his fifteen per cent of the millions I'm going to be paid at the Gunners. Already he can see my bronze statue outside the Emirates, next to Thierry Henry's. Yeah well I'd like that too.

Little brother has changed again. Not so aggressive, just like as mum says to me, he's more like a lodger. He hardly interacts except with mum. He helps mum, cooks, dressed in a frilly apron, making pastry, even making lasagne and takes a pride in it. It's good food; he can even do that well. And annoyingly, his school reports are the opposite of mine. Top of his class in everything except sports where he's just hardly there, picking daisies rather than watching the play in cricket or miss kicking the football. If I miss kicked I'd be embarrassed. He doesn't care at all. He just laughs and when other kids shout at him, he pirouettes. Couldn't care less. He's such an embarrassment. The good thing is, lately he's been doing my homework for me, well helping, teaching. He's bloody clever. That Jenn she's a pretty girl. She has eyes that do all sorts of tricks and a smile that would melt lead soldiers.

Easter hols and luckily dad is home. He sees me play in the last two games of our season and we win two in a row.

Arsenal had a bad stutter in the New Year losing matches they just shouldn't, and then came good on the run in. The fans were yelling for Arsene to go and two months later cheering him. I reckon Arsenal will claim top three and be in Europe next year, again. How Arsene does it I don't know. Being a football manager must be the most stressful of all occupations. He sits there looking glum, weary and then they score and he's flinging himself in the air, punching the breeze, pirouetting. Next minute he's glum as hell if the opposition score. I don't think I could do that.

It's brilliant dad being home. We feel so much more like a family when it's the four of us.

Back to work for dad. He's in the North Sea again, saturation diving after two years as dive master. Not enough activity there for everyone, so they take what's on offer, he says, he hopes next year to get rig captain. He has passed all the exams. So it's a month at sea living in a pod and doing an eight-hour shift on maintenance or something deep down with two other guys and a safety diver up in the bell in case there's trouble. They breathe a helium mixture so they don't get the bends. Sounds awful. An eight-hour shift down there. How do they, you know, go to the toilet? I don't ask.

Back at school and it's cricket. I bat at number six and dad says I need to practice. We go to the nets on the recreation ground.

Cricket's not as good as football for me but I bowl so I always sort of feature. Slow off break and I get five wickets in the first match. The next match they hit me out of the ground and I'm taken off. The ball wouldn't turn at all.

Monday and I wake with a headache and I feel nauseous. I tell mum. She looks at me, hard because I'm never ill, unlike the brat.

She feels my forehead. I'm hot. She puts me in the car and takes me to the surgery, demands to see a doctor and we wait half an hour. He says it's a virus. Bed and paracetamol. I'm home and in bed and mum comes in with pills and a glass and jug of water.

'Oh God. You've got a rash.' She says and I'm immediately in a panic. I've never had a rash.

She puts this glass on my flesh and the rash stays just where it is. 'Up, get up. We're going to hospital.'

Mum gets me dressed and my head is splitting and I'm burning up. 'Mum,' I say. I didn't know I could feel this rotten. She get's me sort of dressed and down the stairs and out into the car and I'm feeling it's freezing, and although it's summer she has the heater on. We drive like mad, she's hitting the horn and the emergency lights are on and we almost jump some lights and she pulls right into Emergency. She runs in and then reappears with two guys in white coats and a nurse. I'm in a wheelchair and rushed through. This doctor looks at me, he does the glass thing and feels my head and I'm feeling really dizzy, and my head is splitting. Mum is tearful, frightened and I know I'm really ill. Next I know I'm being stripped of my clothes and they put this like nightshirt on me and I'm in bed and they're wheeling the bed and I sort of see the ceiling with those spray things if there's a fire, seeming to whiz by…………

A Mum's Tale

Chapter 1.   A Mum's Tale

It's not easy being a mum. Nine months in which time you lose your sylph like figure if you have one to start with. In that time if you're like me, you have morning sickness, some don't; they're the lucky ones. Some have it so badly they almost die. I just had it mildly I suppose.

The drive to reproduce, to hold that precious baby in your arms is an instinct in every animal on this earth. From elephants to the smallest mouse, every mammal has this nurturing instinct. Some women are able to resist it for whatever reason. One thing for sure, it mucks up our lives and one never knows whether the baby will be healthy or happy.

I was watching a programme about the Marsh Lions, a group of lions in East Africa living in a marshy area and the females all cooperate, hunting, nursing the young. The male does nothing except snarl. I sometimes think, men are like that. My husband is fine with Nick but poor Ed. If anything happened, I would never remarry.

Nicholas was an easy baby, fed well, and hardly cried. He was an easy toddler too; just as well because he was not quite three when number two came along. Another boy though I wished for a girl. Edward was as different from his brother as it was possible to be. Cried it seemed for the first nine months of his life. He walked later, not till he was fifteen months but was talking by that time, I mean more than da da; he used intelligible words. He was a pretty baby and there aren't many of them really. Most look like Winston Churchill. I was talking to my doctor the other day, about being a doctor and babies and how every baby is described as beautiful.

Supposed to be that is.

She's a friend so speaking as a friend, she laughed at that. 'I know what you mean. I have a thing about vaginas, I mean they are mostly pretty disgusting. I do it because it's the job. I was examining a woman the other day and I thought, oh that's quite nice, not too bad at all. Yes, It's like that with babies.'

Edward was beautiful, so was Nick but Edward was just something else. After that first nine months, he became an easy baby and then toddler. He got to three and he was so intelligent, making real sentences, not just saying why, why. He was reading at four, picked it up just like that and kept developing. And then it was as though a cloud descended. He was humourless. At playschool he always played with the girls and with the girls' toys. We tried giving him boy toys and

30

he said thank you and we never saw them again. His treasure is his teddy. Still. Moth eaten now, its fur is rubbing off but even at ten years old, he won't part with it. Always sleeps with teddy. Mr Bunkins. Where he got the name from no one knows.

He still sucks his thumb. We tried everything and told him off, quinine other stuff that tastes or smells evil, but he snuggles down in bed and just his eyes are showing and I say take that thumb out. His eyes glint and I know there's a smile there and the thumb is in the mouth. He's so lovable, but a closed book. Nick is an open book, says whatever comes into his head and has no fear of exposing himself, even tossing off the criticisms of his reports.

Edward can't stand his brother, barely stands his father. As time has gone by, a chasm has developed in the family and Edward stays on one side, their father and Nick on the other. I stand in the middle somewhere, prepared to catch Edward. For all he is a clever little boy, I think he needs much more help in this World.

When he was five and went to infants' school, the teachers were worried because he hardly associated with the boys. He was with the girls and played girl's games, skipping and dancing, hop scotch, even the girls slapping, clapping games. Oh he seemed happy but some of the boys gave him a hard time. They asked if he was a boy. He said apparently right back, 'Do I look like a girl?'

They said no. He said, 'Well then.'

He looks like a girl now. He absolutely refuses to have his hair cut.

His dad's disappointed. He was so proud of Nick, who played sport and shows so much promise, yet Nick didn't read until seven and then it was only because he wanted to read about Thierry Henry, the footballer. Nicky asked me to read it to him and I said no we'd read it together. You read what you can and I'll help fill in the gaps. From there we moved on to other things. Cricket. Bikes, he was into them. And then it was motor racing. Seeing it on the TV and reading the live comments on the Internet.

Edward was just so different. Sucked up knowledge, always had his head in a book or his laptop. I walk into Nicky's room and it's a mess. If the bed has been made it's been thrown together, clothes on the floor, a dirty plate and an empty cup or glass.

Edward's room is spotless. His bed is always pristine, there's no dust. His clothes draws are neat and the wardrobe, everything hung up. And yes, as his brother says, it's not really a boy's room, just tiny touches, ornaments he bought at the jumble, one of my silk scarves tied on a draw handle. He even takes my used perfume bottles and lines them up, 'collecting'. It's so worrying. I wonder whether he's going to be gay.

What really worries me is he's so withdrawn. I mean there are only rare glimpses of joy. Then his face lights. That smile would melt the scowl on Jeremy Clarkson's face. He's so beautiful; I could hug him all the time, if he would let me. I'm practically the only one of the family he still has time for and in his way, I'm sure he loves me. We do spend time together, cooking, and he will also do the washing, sorting it and doing the different washes, sometimes asking me which wash I think? When Dad and Nick aren't around we are very close and he is so sweet, so darling.

He will always help me out. He'll vacuum, anywhere in the house except his brother's room. He said, 'No, I'm not going in there, he's a pig. Give him a bucket of swill and he'd paddle in it. I'll do anything else mum but not his room.'

He cooks with me and he's a good cook. His pastry is much better than mine and when he made bread, it was really nice. When I made bread it was more like a breezeblock. He changes his bed although it must be a struggle for a child his size. He has this calendar and on it his day for linen change. He gets through six towels a week.

His hair is now down his back. Actually refuses to have it cut and there are no threats I haven't used, no carrots offered that will convince him to let the scissors at it. Finally I did say split ends and got Rebecca to say so too, so he let her trim the ends. That was only about an inch. I said any longer and I'd have to plait it. He smiled.

I love him so much but he's so annoying. How can one child be so different from the next? Nick is such a boy and boys have annoying ways. Edward is the opposite and almost perfect with me, but utterly horrid to his dad and brother.

His relationship with his dad is practically non-existent. Edward seems to have no respect for his father and his father has no respect for him. I have rowed with his father when he called him 'that Sissy'. Whatever the future, whether Edward is gay or not, he's our son and I will do my best for him, whatever his needs are. But he is such a worry.

Chapter 2.   A Mum's Tale

I keep thinking that with age, Edward will change.

At six I just thought it was a phase and although his teacher spoke highly of his academic performance, she said it was worrying that he seemed not to identify with boys and totally ignored boys in the main.

I took little notice. Children do go through phases. I've spoken to mothers whose boy's cross-dressed and they have turned out to be ordinary boys. Particularly at puberty boys change a lot and I just thought eventually he would come round and recognise he's a boy and like doing boy things. He doesn't.

Another thing, the most worrying thing with Edward. As a small child he had a penchant for dressing up in my clothes. They were of course absurdly large on a seven year old. Then after I told him to leave my things alone, he'd laddered expensive, £17 brand new tights, that all finished. But I would find, things, my best panties amongst his underwear, a pair of tights at the back of his sock drawer. But he doesn't cross dress either, well not any more. He stopped when he was about six or seven and I asked a consultant about it at the University Hospital where I work and he just said, not to worry, he will grow out of it more than likely. And he has.

Still there are those signs in his room the scarf and the ornaments, even flowers which he changes every third day. I said about not having flowers in the room at night. He asked why? I said it was something to do with oxygen levels and he said, "old wife's tale mum.' He had looked it up on his laptop of course.

Then there's his extreme tidiness for a boy. Oh and why should being tidy be thought a female trait? As Barbara Johnson a work mate said, her girls, particularly Rachelle, are dreadful, everything on the floor and just walked over.

I can't remember when he last spoke to his father. If his father orders, I should says requests, Edward to do something, he will either do it without any protest or, he will just disappear. I fear the disdain is mutual. That his father has called him a sissy, cannot be endearing to a child. I can't understand a father saying that to his son, deliberately hurtful because Edward doesn't conform to ones ideal. In so many ways when I really add everything up, Edward is the child many would value above any other. He is pretty, not handsome as yet, very clever, well mannered except when provoked and clean and tidy. He's just not one of the boys and I suspect he never will be.

When we are alone, just he and I, in the kitchen, or shopping, or out for a walk when Nick and his dad have gone to football, he is so endearing, so interested in nature, in the beauty of his surroundings and the history of things. He can tell me when so and so happened like when we were at the local National Trust mansion that was once owned by an Earl. He told me all about it and on the tour, I think he sorely tested the guide. Annoying perhaps, but his brain, he just sucks up knowledge.

We went to the climbing wall on Nick's birthday and of course one can't exclude a brother from a birthday celebration. Where Edward goes so does Jenny, so she was the token female at the party.

Nick climbed the wall in double quick time, just as I knew he would. He thinks he's James Bond or some such character, likes a bit of danger and he's good at anything physical. The other boys went up with mixed success. Then it was Edward's turn. He dropped off at ten feet. He was white as a sheet and in tears.

Surprisingly and before I could jump in and rescue him, he starts to climb again. Nick wanted him brought down, because Ed was obviously terrified. The instructor said no, rightly as it turned out. Edward made it to the top.

When he was lowered down, he was still white, still tears in his eyes but he was smiling. I was so proud, more proud than watching Nick go up in double quick time. My younger son's accomplishment was all the more praiseworthy because he had conquered his fear. I told my husband and he just sniggered. Unforgiveable.

I told Rebecca and she agreed. She likes Nick, says he's a handsome boy but she loves Edward. She says that if she could choose either as her son, it would be Edward.

I went into his room yesterday. A silk scarf sent me from America by his aunt Susan, was tied to his drawer handle.

Then there's his meticulous hygiene, washing and tooth brushing. I know with his teeth, he has a brace, so he has to make a special effort, but he seems to spend hours in the bathroom while Nick is in and out in five minutes.

I detected my perfume on him too. I told his father.

'It's your fault,' he said, 'molly coddled that child from the time he was born. Turned him into a sissy. I've no patience with him, no time for a cry-baby.'

'So you've written off one of your children because he's not your ideal? He'll go far in whatever field he goes into, probably be a professor of something and yet, you haven't time for him? I think that's a disgusting thing to say. I didn't treat him any differently to Nick. How would you know, you were never bloody well here?'

'I was at the bottom of the bloody ocean, that's what, keeping you in dresses.'

'You really are a stupid man. You have no idea do you? You can't or won't cook, even though I'm out to work. You never do anything around the house. Your attempts at gardening are beans and rhubarb and a bit of mowing, and you take the car to the car wash. Oh yes, you play with Nick but take absolutely no interest in our clever, bookish son at all.'

'I'm a good provider......'

'And a lousy lover.' I walk out. I bang pots and pans onto the stove, ready for tonight's meal when my boys come home from their different schools. My eyes fill with tears and I cry silently.

I look up the garden and see Rebecca drive in with Jenn and Ed. I walk up and through into their garden.

'Hi Lizzie. Here he is, do you want him?'

'Not at the moment. I wouldn't mind a cuppa if you're having one?'

'Of course. You two, are you doing homework or playing.'

'Playing.'

'OK then.'

We enter her kitchen, a similar layout to ours but they have a new marble top while ours is wood. She fills the teapot from the instant boiling water tap.

She puts biscuits on the table and two mugs and a jug of milk.

'Jenn, you two! A drink come and get it please.'

She pours milk into the Shake mixer and a packet. The machine buzzes crazily and produces a pink frothy liquid.

My son enters the kitchen followed by Jenn. They look so happy. They collect a glass each and Edward says, 'Thank you Rebecca.' 'Thanks mum,' from Jenn.

'Off you go then kids. What are you doing?'

'Glitter tattoos mum.'

'Show me.'

Edward pulled his sleeve up. He had a glittering red heart on his arm. He smiled. And came closer to show me.

'That's something else,' I say and they run off giggling.

Rebecca is watching me. She raises her eyebrows. 'That's how they are all the time when they're together.'

'I know. It's just lovely to see Edward happy. I hope he's not here too much. I worry when I see him heading up the garden and through the gate to yours.'

'I love him as my own Lizzie, you know I do. The child I never had and such good company for Jenn. I don't think there will be wedding bells though.'

'Well it's early to think of that.'

'That's not what I meant. Edward is not going to be, oh how do I say this, marriageable.'

'What do you mean?'

'He's either gay or have you thought, trans, transgender or transsexual, gender neutral; the terminology defeats me. These days as soon as a name is put to something, it's designated as incorrect or non PC and another definition comes up.'

'Well I've had this conversation with John.'

'What does he say. I guess a bit negative.'

'A bit! Talks about Sissies he doesn't want to hear about Edward, just picks up the 'Pink Un' and reads about football, as though he would find the answer there.'

'But you've thought about it?'

'Of course. I've watched one or two programmes on TV. Tried to get John to watch. He wouldn't. That macho diving environment he lives in, they don't understand anything other than straight and don't want to, even though it's his son we are discussing.'

'Head in the sand! What are you going to do?'

'I keep wondering, hoping he will grow out of it, that it's a phase.'

'It's been a long phase.'

'Yes, when you say that, ever since he was four or five. Rebecca, I'm so frightened of putting ideas in his head. That's why I haven't confronted him. I don't know what to do. If I ask if he would rather have been a girl, will that set him on the path to being trans? Not that there's anything wrong with that, but we know, gay, trans anything other than straight, is not an easy option. Trans is the most difficult of all.'

'Yes. Have you thought of getting professional help?'

'What?'

'Well a counsellor or psychiatry, your GP?'

'It's getting to that stage. It's splitting the family. I think if he turns out to be trans, it will end my marriage. There's no way that John will come to terms with it.'

'And Nick?'

'Oh he's OK. He doesn't understand what's going on with little brother, but he's quite good with him under sometimes, severe provocation. Edward frequently destroys Nick with his tongue. The next minute he's helping with Nick's homework. Nick is not a dunce, just doesn't try. His father's son; he thinks everything except kicking a ball a waste of time.

'Edward has this way of looking at people, what Nick calls his power eyes, if he thinks he's being victimised or you're wrong, it's as though he really can't understand and is trying to look into your brain. Either that or it's just plain hate.'

'I've never seen that. He's so happy here with Jenn. You would think they're identical twins, never an argument. Liz, he is very girlie, does everything she does except wear her clothes. He sit's to pee!'

'How do you know?'

'He told Jenn and she told me. She was innocently amused.'

43

'Does that mean something? It is more hygienic than boys and men splashing all over the place with their hosepipes.'

Rebecca laughed. 'Yes you're right there, but is it normal?'

'Rebecca, I'm not going to promote a state of mind in him by asking outright.'

'What if I ask Jen to?'

'Not yet, please not yet. He is only nine.'

'Yes. There's time. But it has to be before puberty, before his looks are damaged and his voice changes. I've seen programmes. If he is trans, then the sooner a change the better, certainly before puberty. You realise that?'

'Then I guess I have about eighteen months.'

'Anyway, he's welcome here anytime for as long as. I do love him as my own and he's such good company for Jenny. Come and chat any time.'

'Rebecca, this is an awful thing to say, an unbearable thought. If anything happened to John and me, we died, would you have our boys? I can't think of anyone better, and of course there would be money to keep them.'

'Of course. That's such a great compliment. Are you going to make that legal? You would need to put that in your will and perhaps we need to write a letter to attach, agreeing. I would when I think about it, like to reciprocate with Jenny, just in case. One never knows.'

'No one doesn't. Of course. Jenn and Ed are inseparable.'

'Like twin sisters.'

We both made it legal. We went to the solicitor together. My husband just shrugged.

Chapter 3.   A Mum's Tale.

After the talk with Rebecca, I was more observant with Edward. Now I watched every movement, started searching his room, analysed every little thing, every remark.

I tried talking to his father, but I might as well have tried to tunnel out of a castle with a wooden toothpick. His mind was completely closed to having a son that was anything other than straight, virile, footie playing and beer drinking.

Nick on the other hand was really good. I sat him down while Ed was out with Jenn.

'Dad's right about one thing mum. He is really girly. And he can be so annoying, his power stare is quite frightening and that air of defiance, almost daring me to lash out. I don't know what goes on in his mind. Then I grabbed him the other night and asked him to show me how to do an algebra question for homework and he explained step by step, so even I could understand. If he was my teacher at school, I know I'd do better than now. He's a brainbox and when he's nice, he's so sweet. It's like, I don't know, like he's a cat. You stroke it and then you make one false move and it's no more purr purr, the claws are out and I come away with a scratched face, you know, not actually.'

'Metaphorically.'

'Yeah. Metaphorically.'

'What am I going to do then Nick. Your father has washed his hands. Edward is lovely, I love him as much as I do you, but it's difficult. Do I challenge him; ask why he's like he is? What's troubling him? I spoke to Rebecca. She says he's no trouble up there. Loves having him and he and Jenn are joined at the hip.'

'It's because he's a girl mum. You should get him certified or whatever they do.'

'What if he isn't trans or gay? I don't want to put ideas in his head or get him labelled.'

'Then mum, only time will tell and maybe that will be the worst option. I don't think you can put ideas in his head. Mentally he is far too strong. I mean the climbing wall. He was nearly wetting himself but he did it. I did find something.'

'What do you mean?'

'I was in his room and he'd left his laptop on. No I don't want to tell you. It's like spying.'

'You have to say.'

'It was all statistics. One of the things was I'm trying to get it right, undiagnosed, that means people having something but not knowing?'

'Yes roughly.'

'Undiagnosed or prevented from treatment. A fifty per cent suicide rate in trans people.'

'Fifty per cent? That's ridiculous.'

'That's what it said, but then that was in the USA. Might be a lot different here.'

'That's frightening if right. No, he's too happy. It's only here, his dad he hates. I know he does and its mutual between them.'

'I don't think he hates dad, not really. He want's his dad to show some affection. He said to me, Dad hates me. He does.'

'No not hate. He just doesn't understand how a son of his can not be, well the same as you Nick.'

Nick shrugged as though he thought I was wrong. I hope I'm not.

Christmas. We spend a lot of time, all Christmas day with the Jennings, theirs for Christmas lunch, a proper traditional lunch with the Queen's broadcast with the pudding, then back to ours for recovery followed by Christmas supper, cold meats, salad, sautéed potatoes or potato salad and pickles, washed down with champagne. The kids play

Monopoly. In the end they give up, tired of the game before a winner is established.

That's Christmas over. I've made my mind up. If Ed is still the same by summer holiday and his move to senior school in September, I'm asking him if he's gay or trans. I can't wait any longer.

I tell Rebecca, and John. 'Well it's a plan at least.' Rebecca says. I think she believes I should have grasped this nettle long ago, for Edward's sake.

Chapter 3.   A Mum's Tale

Work is not what it was in the hospital. Back room staff like me are not well respected. Nor are the nurses for that matter. The upper echelon, the top brass are paid exorbitant amounts for mismanaging. Our chief executive is on over two hundred thousand plus bonuses. Bonuses? For what? For not doing what she should be doing on that exorbitant salary anyway. But she is failing and if it goes on, the whole pack of cards will come falling down.

I went to see one of the shrinks. I asked about helping a mythical friend, asking whether a child should be challenged about his/her sexuality or orientation, being gay or trans. He asked the age and when I said at nine or ten, he said no. One has to wait for them to make their mind up. He said that during puberty they often changed their minds.

I'm still not sure but at least I have asked advice from someone who is supposed to know. I don't see that Ed will suddenly become masculine, even inclined to be masculine. He is really fussy with his clothes. They have to be immaculate.

Anyway, one good thing is that Nick has a good, well better report for this spring term. I can't help thinking that it is the coaching from his brother that's made the difference. Edward has spent hours with him I find and yet his own marks are still the best in the class. Top again. My clever boy. His father passed no comment.

The Easter holidays are here. School holidays are always a trial and John tries to be home while I still go to work. John is home until after the Easter break and he flies out to the rig the Wednesday after school term begins. At least that is the holiday covered. I guess anyway that Ed will be with Jenny most of the time.

In term time, it's almost better without John, though Nick misses his dad. Still Nick has so many friends he can amuse himself. He and his band are practising at Sean's house where Sean's dad has turned the garage into a practice room with sound proofing so the neighbours are not annoyed with screaming guitars and banging of drums. Nick plays the piano here a lot too and his father found a second hand Roland Synthesiser, which now lives over in the garage now called 'the studio'. 'Mum, I'm going to the studio,' and off he cycles guitar in its case over his back. Here Nick just has the piano and that I don't mind at all.

Edward is with the Jennings, on holiday for a week away. So life is easy. When he returns I don't have to worry, he is off to Jenn's every day after breakfast and with just dad here, he doesn't return until I come home. I spoke to Rebecca about it and she said she loved having him and what a dear he is and how happy those two are together. It's almost unbelievable. They seem true soul mates. All children seem to have fallings out but not Jenn and Edward. They just love each other's company.

Jenn dressed Ed as her twin. They were both in almost identical tops and different coloured peddle pushers and pumps. Rebecca said that he was completely unblushing, just giggled and held Jenn's hand. He stayed like it all day, one of Jenn's slides in his hair, only changing to come home.

Do I say something? I asked if he'd had a nice day and he said great. What did you do? 'Nothing much mum, went shopping just the supermarket.'

I tell Nick. He just says, 'Typical. Don't expect he looked anymore girly than usual.'

Yes but it is a new development, a further sign. What boy would allow that? Most would shy away immediately. Real boys hate to be associated with anything feminine don't they? I confess I'm all at sea here. My knowledge of the male is really restricted to my dad, my husband, a few ex boyfriends and my children. It's not exactly a firm basis of research. I spent time in the hospital library looking for things on transgender. There was nothing. People I speak to, seem to have entrenched ideas based, when one examines their judgements, on intuition and prejudice. Will Edward grow out of his girly ways, will puberty make him male? I wish I knew.

At last it's back to school and I'm so relieved. Monday morning and I watch Ed walk up to the Jennings to go with her to school, their last term in the juniors.

I shout Nick and he appears his clothes array and he says he doesn't feel well. First, god forgive me, I think he is swinging the lead because he doesn't want to go to school. I feel his forehead and he's warm. I ask his symptoms? Boys are so useless at telling how they feel. Achy he says. Where?

'My head mum.'

I get him in the car, and we are off to the surgery to see the GP. I phone work saying I'll be late in. We wait for thirty minutes and see a registrar. He does all the tests; I must say he was pretty thorough young man. He says it's a virus, but if it gets any worse, to come back.

We return home and he goes up to get into bed. I go up fifteen minutes later with a jug of water and he's developed this rash. I remember something I'd heard. I place the glass on his flesh and press. The rash is supposed to go away but it doesn't. It may not be but I'm terribly frightened it's that dread disease, meningitis.

'Oh Nick, I don't like the look of that. Up get up. Put your dressing gown on, here.' I help him on with it. 'Downstairs and into the car.'

I hang onto him and I can see he's already weak and groggy from a raging fever. We are in the car and I phone the emergency that I'm coming in with a suspected case of meningitis. I have my foot down and I'm passing cars and breaking the speed limit. I switch on my warning flashers and use the horn and Nick says, 'Careful mum, you'll get done,' (for speeding). I don't care.

We arrive at Emergency and I leave him in the car. I rush in and grab George, one of the porters I know and they bring a wheel chair out and Nick is in that and in, immediately seeing the Emergency consultant who's calm but quick. He makes a phone call and then Nick is on his way to a side ward on male surgical the only bed available.

Three medics examine him; they take a blood sample and rush that to the lab. It will take two hours for the analysis.

I phone Rebecca and tell her what's happening and ask if she will keep Edward. Of course she will.

It's confirmed it is meningitis. By this time Nick has been transferred to ICU. I'm gowned up and allowed to enter. Nick's face is red. Machines bleep and I watch as he breathes. I go out and phone Rebecca.

'Don't worry Ed is safe with us for as long as.'

That's what I love about Rebecca; she is always unflappable and seemingly good-humoured. Theirs is a relaxed household, even Peter, her husband appears always good humoured and even tempered.

I phone the rig company. John is down in the bell and they will not pass a message for safety reasons, but they will bring the bell up tomorrow, before schedule and as soon as the job they are on is in a safe state. I tell them his son is gravely ill. They will divert a helicopter to pick him up and he will come the next morning.

I sit in the hospital and wait for news. He's holding his own they say. What does that mean? Evening and nothing new. They find me a cubicle in Emergency where I can sleep. I manage a few hours and wake to the nightmare of reality.

The morning dawns. I go to the staff canteen and some of the staff I know ask why I'm in so early and ask if I'm OK. They know I'm not. I look and feel dishevelled. I tell them about Nick and they are kind but just offer platitudes.

I realise I'm abrupt and distracted. I can't be bothered with them my whole focus is on my boy. I have managed some cornflakes and orange juice and I buy two bottles of water which I stuff in my handbag. I make my way up to ICU.

The consultant visits. They say nothing. I can't see him. He's in this polythene tent. I sit and wait. I ask the nurse and she says the consultant will be coming back.

The consultant, Mr Berry returns.

'It's not good news Mrs Simpson. We are going to amputate both legs and some fingers. We'll save what we can.'

I burst into tears. I'm absolutely helpless. My son is within three metres of me but I can't even touch him let alone save him. For Nick to lose his legs is just the worst thing.

They come for him and he's wheeled out and away to the lift for the theatre floor. I go up in the lift with him and I sit outside in the corridor. Within five minutes, they tell me Nick is dead. How can that be? My golden fit virile boy has gone. I break down and a nurse does her best to comfort me.

I phone Rebecca. She comes with Peter. She drives me home and Peter drives my car.

I phone John. I lie that Nick is very ill. I can't let him drive home with the news that his son is dead. Even this news he takes really badly.

Chapter 4.   A Mum's Tale

John arrives home and I break the news. I couldn't tell him the details over the phone, I tell him because I thought it would be dangerous as he was driving. He can get in such a temper.

As one might expect, he takes it really badly. He blames me. He says without any foundation, I was so preoccupied with Edward that I missed the signs that Nick was ill. The facts are that there were no signs until Nick came down that Monday morning, the first day of term. Within three hours of Nick telling me he felt ill, he was in hospital. Twenty-four hours later, he was dead. What more could I have done.

John won't see reason and to make it worse, he takes it out on Edward, curses him and makes him cry. Edward's little face crumples and he runs out of the house and back to Jenn's. I follow.

Rebecca says he can stay with them until John has got over the shock. That's all right, but I need my son, I need Edward. He's all I have left. My marriage seems to be foundering. The death of Nick is the last thread of the rope that holds John and I together.

We hardly speak after the first discussion of where we go from here. Then he comes in one morning, when Ed has gone to school. He accuses me of spending all my time on 'that sissy'. 'I don't believe he's even my child,' John says.

'Oh don't be so ridiculous John. If you had listened to anything I said or read anything, you would know that anyone in this world could have a trans child. It all happens in the womb. Reproduction is not guaranteed, babies are produced with defects every day and transsexualism is a defect caused in the womb by a chemical imbalance.'

He won't see reason. He just slammed out of the house. He came in just as it was getting dark. He'd been to the golf range and then the club bar. He must have driven home drunk. I told him that he wouldn't be employed as a diver if they thought he had a drink problem. He has to sober up too, because he has his diving medical and they don't pass that easily. I say we have a date for the funeral, three weeks time at the Crematorium.

'I may not be there.'

'Where will you be? What do you mean, you won't be at Nick's funeral. He's your son!'

'Was my son, was until you let him die. Fuck you. I try to make a good living for us, risking my life under that murky North Sea and you can't even keep him safe.'

I'm stunned that our relationship has so deteriorated.

'There's no reasoning with you John. You need to see a counsellor or someone. Go to the GP.'

'It's not me needs the counselling; it's your brat, the Sissy Boy always playing his girlie games. You're so protective of him and you let a proper boy die.'

I say no more. What would be the point of discussing with someone so deranged? I'm just as heartbroken. I go into the twilight of this spring evening and sit on the garden swing, just moving it back and forth. I'm crying, sat there, feeling a failure and it's no use anyone telling me, it's not my fault, these diseases strike with no apparent reason. I'm bereft. I'm so alone. Just when I really need John, and God knows he hasn't really been that much of a husband, he has rejected me.

I'm depressed, I realise that much. I sleep in Nick's room. I shall not sleep again with John. I don't think I can come back to him after this.

In the morning I go and see the GP. He's concerned, not just for me but for the whole family. He sits close before me and holds my hands. He calls the nurse in and I breakdown completely. He prescribes some tablets and writes a sick note to commence from the last day of my bereavement leave.

There's work to do in the house and my remaining son to look after. Edward is very clingy. He spends every minute with me or with Jenny when his father is in the house. I'm afraid his relationship with his father is at the lowest ebb. John only has to appear and Ed's face crumples. The atmosphere is unbearable.

John takes off. I have gone to buy food and come back to a note. He's gone walking in the Fells the area around his boyhood home in County Durham. As though I don't need support.

I have to arrange everything for the funeral. Five days later John returns. He's still no help, just leaves the house early morning and returns to sleep. Where he goes or what he does I don't know. If he can't help me I really can't be bothered with him.

Somehow we get through the next two weeks and we have the funeral. To anyone outside it would look as though we are a united little family mourning one of our two children. John puts on a good act. Oh he is mourning but loving father of Ed and husband to me, he certainly is not. Even allowing for how he doted on Nick, I cannot excuse him.

He goes back to work. The house is so quiet. Edward is quiet, so quiet I fear he has run away or he too has died and I seek him out, just to make sure he is still here.

I think I'll leave Nick's room as he left it and then I think, no if I create a shrine, I shall never put the tragedy behind me. Every time I pass the door, I would be tempted to just go in and sit, pretending he was still there although I'd really know he wasn't. I have to come to terms with his death. He is gone. All that's left of Nick is our memories of him.

While John is on the rig, I clean the room out, clear it completely, even the bed and the bedding, sold by an advert in the local shop and some gone to jumble and charity. Edward and I do a small garage sale until the only thing left is the upright piano in the dining room. I give the boys in the band his guitar and the synthesiser.

When John comes home, he's dismayed that all Nick's things are gone. 'It's no good dwelling on the past.' I say. 'We still have photos.'

'You're so hard.' He replies.

I don't bother to reply. If he thinks that, then he doesn't know me at all.

I don't see much of him. He goes to the golf club or for a run. I'm back at work and Edward is at school.

Edward has an afternoon off for the dentist because the brace on his teeth needs adjustment. We go to the dentist and that's all fine. Edward is still very quiet but things between he and I are excellent. It's more like old times and he is my baby again. Oh I am not as much fun as Jenny, that of course is understandable.

'So would you say you are boy and girlfriend?' I ask.

'Just friends, that's all mum. She's my best friend.'

Edward is pushing the trolley. He bangs into the fruit counter, without damaging anything and I fly off the handle. 'Don't be so stupid Edward.'

His little face that had been smiling seems to fall apart and I see that look, the intense penetrating gaze that I think is one of puzzlement, trying to make sense of the world.

'I just wanted to choose the apples mum. I didn't mean to.' After that he's offering advice and suggesting, 'Do we need this? Can we get that? That's on offer mum.'

God forgive me, I bark at him and he leaves me, runs out of the shop. I finish the shopping and go through check out having loaded my bags myself and put them back in the cart to take to the car. It has all seemed like extra hard work.

I push the trolley and find him sat on one of the window ledges. He's been crying.

'Thank you Edward, when I really need you, you run off.'

We walk to the car. He puts his right hand on the trolley. At the car I unload our bags into the boot and he runs off with the trolley to the trolley park.

When he gets in the car, he says, 'Mum why don't you love me.'

'I do love you.'

'You never hug me. Never kiss me. Dad hates me. Do you hate me too?'

My heart nearly breaks. 'How can you say that?'

'There's no warmth in our house. At least when Nick was here someone loved someone.'

'I do love you, of course I do. Every day I do things for you, that's love.'

'That's not what the Internet says, it's duty. I do lots too, like I want to help and I don't have to. I do because I love you. Then you shout at me in the Supermarket, I was hurt mum, when I was so happy helping. I hate my life. I wish I lived with Jenn.'

'You're there too much.' I'm jealous that he compares me to Rebecca. At the same time I realise he's right. He has absolutely no love from his father and our failing marriage has sent me into a downward spiral.

'I go there for warmth mum. Jenn and I are like sisters, I mean she's my sister.'

He's slipped up and shown me how he thinks of himself. I lean across the gear lever and grasp him. I kiss his head. 'I worry about you all the time Ed. I know you're not happy. I know your dad and I, well, we're not getting on. I wonder now if we ever will. Nick was the cement between us. Now your dad has no one.'

'He could love me mum, but he doesn't. I hate him.'

He bursts into tears and I cry too. It's five minutes before I can see properly, to start the car and drive home. Dad's car is not there.

Two weeks later, the weekend before John goes back to work. It's breakfast and as usual, if Ed says anything to his father, John just grunts.

Edward knocks the sugar bowl and John tears into him. I have to stop it. I'm in tears and Edward is in tears. Life is unbearable. I have washed the wooden spoon I use for porridge. I hit John across the wrist with it. He looks at me as if I've gone crazy and I think for a second he will retaliate. He has risen from the table. He walks out.

John clears off to golf, again. He ought to live there in a bunker or whatever they call it. In the afternoon because Ed is in such a state, we go to the cinema. The choice is between Star Wars or the Secret of Moonacre, a really girlie film. Of course he chooses Moonacre.

He really enjoys it, grips my hand in some parts and he's excited in others.

We do the supermarket shop on the way home. He is so good, fetching stuff and being careful, helping me load. We reach home and John's car is in the drive, yet the house looks closed.

I unload and Edward is there, carrying bags in after I've unlocked the door. We go through with the bags of groceries to the kitchen. There's a note on the table addressed to me. I think John has been called back to work. I open it and I know immediately from the length that it's more than that. I go up to our bedroom and read. John has left us, for good. He makes that clear, he's not coming back. He will send money he says.

Edward comes in having found me. 'I put everything away mum.'

I look at him. This pretty little boy with the long golden blond hair down to his shoulders. I haven't given him enough attention, enough love. Nick was so easy to love, so straightforward. Ed needed me and I let him down. If it hadn't been for Rebecca and Jenny he would have had no one. I wonder where the two of us are going, how we will survive.

'Thank you Edward. You're such a good kid.'

'Has dad gone to work?'

'Dad's left us. A job in Mexico.'

'But he'll come back?'

'No dear. He's gone, he's not coming back.'

I pull him to me. I hug him and I kiss him. Yes I have not done that enough. Perhaps if I had, he would have had the confidence to tell me what troubles him. I'm convinced now, that he sees himself not just as a girl but also as Jenn's sister. Poor, poor, boy. How useless I've been as a mother. How useless as a wife.

'Why not go and see your sister. Ask if you can stay the night. I have things to do here. Before you go, come here.'

I pull him in close. He radiates heat as children seem to do. Automatically I feel his forehead. I'm now over-protective, fearing another case of meningitis. He feels quite normal.

'If you could choose boy or girl, which would you be?'

He turns red and I know the answer before he speaks. 'Mummy, I have a girl brain, that's why I like doing girl things.'

'Edward, always remember this. I have always loved you, always, from the minute you were born, no before, when you were inside me. I would rub my belly with you inside, thinking about you and how you'd be. I'm so proud of you. So proud. You are beautiful, clever, sensitive, a loving child without a bad bone. I'm sorry that so much time has been spent on Nick and his pursuits over the years, while you were showing us how brilliant you are. Always remember, even if I haven't been so demonstrative, I loved every bone in your body, hair on your head even your sweet breath.' I kiss him long and hard. 'Now go and see Jenn and Rebecca.'

Chapter 1.   Saskia's Tale

As I write this, I'm sitting in my room in Downing College, University, in that loveliest of University cities, Cambridge. I would like to say first of all, I loved my dad. He was a good man, a hard worker. He worked on the rigs in the North Sea or I should say, under them, deep in the ocean, so he was away three or four weeks at a time.

Dad was I suppose what they call a man's man. Oh he liked women, but his passion was doing manly things. I mean his work for a start in the oil industry, a roustabout who worked his way up, becoming eventually drill captain and then taking all his marine exams so he would qualify as Rig Captain. That's what he does now, out in the Gulf of Mexico. I hear from him very occasionally, a short letter, hoping that I'm well and a little about his life, his Mexican American wife and two children, a boy and a girl. I have a photo of them on my desk.

I also have a photo of my mum and of my adopted family, Peter and Rebecca, adoptive parents and of course, one of my beautiful sister, Jenn, Jenny.

How it happened that they adopted me is a really long story. After all the trauma of my early years when I hardly knew who I was, the last six years have been wonderful. Life has been better than I could ever have imagined it would be eight years ago when we were all so unhappy.

Joining the Jennings family was like, well, coming home. They understood me, understood my needs and vowed they would do everything to help me find happiness and they kept that vow.

So here I am, Cambridge University, one of the best Colleges, Downing. It's about four hundred metres from the Mall, just off Regent Street. It's like walking into an oasis when one turns in through the iron gates and past the porters lodge. The lawns are well kept, the buildings are beautiful, especially the Library and the refectory too, well all of it.

My room is more or less the same as Jenn's although she's in a building the other side of the courtyard. It's like a hotel room, single bed, a desk and a couple of chairs and a tiny kitchenette and a bathroom. It's actually luxurious by student standards. Because we are in college, we have to maintain standards, no weird decoration, or sellotape all over the wall. No smoking but that doesn't bother us, who smokes these days?

So that's me. Studying hard and working to be a doctor. I thought, well if I can't have children, then being a doctor for them, a paediatrician would be the next best thing. Maybe I will get the chance to adopt a child, either one from here in England, God knows there are enough mistreated kids here or one from abroad, from one of the awful war zones, like at the moment, Syria. If that is still going on when I'm qualified, I will join MSF and work with them for a time, giving back in a small way. I hope by then they will have found peace. I have to say, I blame men, men wanting power or wanting to keep power. It the old rutting deer syndrome but with humans it seems to be always, the innocent who suffer most.

Now I need to go back in time and explain just how I come to be here. Oh there's Jenny and her boy friend, I wonder where they're going? Oh coming here by the look of it. Jenn is studying chemical engineering, so we do biology, maths and chemistry together, but she also does computer science and some physics.

I open the door so they can just walk in. James her boyfriend is what one would call chiselled, craggy looks, very manly, but from a nice family in Yorkshire and studying law like Jenn.

'Hi we're going for Pizza and we want you to come. Larry is coming too so come on, you can't be stuck in your books all the time.'

'I'm not, I'm writing, about my life, about you Jenn and my family.'

'That can wait then. Come.'

'Makeup, two minutes.'

I go in the bathroom and give my pale eyebrows and lashes some colour.

'Ready.' I sling a tiny bag across my chest and slip my sandals on. 'Let's go sis.'

I close my laptop and the window and lock it. There have been things go missing.

James is waiting for us in the courtyard. We walk through town to our favourite place. It looks like a Roman Temple from the outside. We enter and are shown through to our table. There's a young man sitting with his back to the door. I'm nervous; I always am when meeting new people. I know it's silly, because Jenn has told me often enough, oh and Rebecca and my dad Simon and even my real dad who I last saw two years ago, that there is nothing about me that says boy. Luckily I was given T blockers early enough to rescue me from male development.

Chapter 2.   Saskia's Tale

I'm telling you how it was eight years ago. I'll try and get it all right, but some of it's a bit hazy and it was so traumatic, it gets mixed up in my mind, particularly the sequence of events. I'll try to tell it as I saw life at that time.

When he was home, Dad took us places, amused us, mainly my brother Nick actually. He picked us up from school, well if he wasn't playing golf or going to football. He was a supporter of the Arsenal and he would sometimes go to see their matches and take my brother too because Nick, unlike me, was really into sport and he was also a promising footballer. That's what dad thought anyway.

When Nick moved to big school, I was only eight. Jenn's mum Rebecca picked me up and I used to stay there and do my homework and wait till mum came home. Dad didn't have much to say to me anyway.

It's not that he excluded me, but after I had refused to go to Arsenal a few times, he didn't bother asking again. I went that first time and I found it quite frightening, the crush first of all and the drunk people and the very male atmosphere, expressed either in mild aggression or sometimes excessive male ebullience and brotherliness. Sometimes there was just open aggression, a few punches thrown in a drunken brawl.

I think I was eight when I went with them to the Emirates. As we left I got sort of crushed between two men and banged in the face with an elbow. That's when I realised that men take up a lot of room in this world and for the most part, seem oblivious of those around them. They just looked down at me from six feet to my three feet something and squashed me again as they swung together. Dad then decided he better keep a hold of me and we walked hand in hand. That wasn't the only reason I never went again. I found the whole thing quite frightening and foreign, tribal.

I would rather watch it on TV, where one sees a sanitized version, insulated from the passion and violence of the crowd. Even on TV I find it all rather nasty, especially some of the players. There's one player I really like, Theo Walcott who seems to be a gentleman as well as talented. He's also quite good looking.

Football fans amongst you will just dismiss me as a sissy. I don't think so; it's not a sissy thing. Like I can watch hockey or even rugby and though of all games rugby is a very hard game, it's not horrid. Footballers play act, trying to have an opposite number penalised. That is cheating, it's not a 'professional foul' or gamesmanship, it's cheating. The referees are not respected, whereas in rugby and hockey, a decision is usually unquestioned. The referee's decision is law. In a real dispute they resort to a televised replay. In football the referees make lots of mistakes because they can't always see, but there's no recourse to replay, so the referees' decisions are suspect.

Then there's all that male kissing and hugging, yet they think they are men? And spitting. Ugh! The beautiful game it is not. I lost Dad's respect because I said what I thought of the football World. Weirdo!

So sort of out of interest and because I was supposed to be a boy, I sort of supported Arsenal. Mr Wenger made me laugh and makes me laugh because in the after match interviews he often seems to have been watching a different game. He must have something to have survived twenty years as a manager.

Back in those days, when I was a pre-teen, I would rather stay at home and help mum or go shopping with her or maybe if it was wet, watch a film like Keira Knightly in Pride and Prejudice. If I could look like anyone, it would be Keira.

Dad worked on the oil and gas rigs. It was dangerous on the rigs and dangerous getting on and off them, helicopters do go down and unfortunately it happened twice last year. Luckily back in those days, eight years ago, dad was safe on his flights.

From the age of I don't know, probably four, maybe even before that, I knew that things were wrong. I was in a family that was not short of money, living in a nice house in a nice street. The neighbours were all nice too, except for old man Hicks at number thirty-one, who had taken it upon himself to be the 'blockleiter' of our street, according to dad who knows about Nazis, those German people under Hitler. Hicks would tell us off for cycling on the pavement or for congregating on our bikes or me, riding my old tricycle over his grass verge.

From that first realisation that my world was askew, life could only get worse as I grew up.

Everything got horrid when I went to school. There were two races of human there, male and female. The problem was I found that I was in the wrong race, I was a boy, a horrid ghastly boy like my beastly brother and I should have been in the other tribe, a girl with pretty hair, in a dress and playing their games.

Luckily I found that Jenny who lived at the bottom of our garden was in the same class and through her I sort of became an honorary girl, playing with the girls at break time, hopscotch, skipping, slapping games that as boys we were not taught but Jenn taught me. Jenn taught me everything. Like peeing. Boys stood aiming their little penises and seeing who could get highest, while girls hitched their skirts and pulled down their knickers and sat and wiped. I did that too.

The boy toys my parents gave me were of little interest. I didn't want cars or footballs, guns, violent computer games. I wanted a dress or a silk scarf, a soft toy. In the end they bought me a real grown up laptop computer and I was set free. With that, I could go anywhere in the known universe, learn anything, investigate, analyse and compare.

By age eight I knew I was transsexual. I would have told my family, but I was already condemned by dad. He called me a sissy boy. I bore no comparison to the prowess of my brother who was manly, sporty, and talented. I might have known the dates of Alfred the Great, AD 849 – 899, that he actually reigned for twenty eight years as King of Wessex, not even England and the burning cakes incident was just a myth, but that hardly compared with scoring a goal.

I ought to have said, at least told mum I was trans. Maybe she would still be here if I had. I can't analyse why I didn't. Fear of dad, idiotic pride or was it shame. I just don't know. Boys are conditioned to be boys at least in our family and it's like shame if they're not like Nick, not a proper boy.

The year from my tenth birthday was a momentous year in our small family. We were outwardly a normal family. Anyone looking from the outside would have seen what some would think the ideal nuclear family, I looked it up on the Net, nuclear nothing to do with bombs, two married parents, both hard working and two boys, my brother just thirteen and me ten and a bit. My dad was an only child, mum's sister is in America, and so we were without uncles or aunts. My grands were all dead by the time I was six. I can hardly remember them.

If one had put our family under a microscope, one would have seen there was a chasm splitting us into two, if not three. I was on one side of the canyon, shy, withdrawn, bookish, continually on my laptop or my head in a reader or a print book. I was secretive and possessed a tongue that even at that young age could lash and smart. I was, now I look back at my world as it was then, at war with everything. My dad was a good man but uneducated. He had made his way in the world, learning what he needed to move up the ladder.

There is nothing wrong with being uneducated as long as one tries to better oneself, that is what one of my English teachers said when he was speaking about Mark Twain considered to be one of America's foremost authors and a great wit. I looked him up on Wiki.

Dad was no Mark Twain but he had started on the oilrigs as a roustabout. Then he went on a diving course and joined the navy and became a diver there. After six years he came out and went as a diver in the North Sea, working under the ocean. He met mum and they married. He became a drill captain and is now a rig captain, in charge of a whole platform. Hard work and study as grand pop used to say, he pulled himself up by his bootstraps.

There are always stroppy teenagers, but I was not that yet. It was no flush of hormones setting me at war with the world; it was having a brain out of kilter with my body.

Mum attempted to bring peace, just as a UN mediator might try to unite a country on the brink of civil war. Mum obviously loved Nick her firstborn. He was a golden boy, easy to love, happy, usually polite, and full of energy and the joy of living. He was good at sport, any sport from table tennis to football. I abhorred sport. I was offered dance but I was too shy, too withdrawn to take that up. I did go riding and I liked a good hack but I wasn't interested in jumping or the finer points. I didn't even particularly like horses. They are rather stupid creatures. Why else would they allow a human to ride on their backs or hit them with a whip? A dog would turn, a cat that size would tear you limb from limb.

Nick was the apple of Dad's eye. They did a lot together, laughed together and even swapped notes on girls they saw in the street. Even at thirteen and a bit, Nick had a way with the girls, a confidence far beyond his years and they liked this open, polite boy who spoke to them so naturally.

My parents tried to draw me in. I would do things reluctantly except for helping about the house. I didn't mind that at all. I loved to be in the kitchen, making food that was a delight to the senses. Mum was a good cook and taught me lots. From the age of four I stood on a footstool peeling potatoes or apples, I made pastry. I knew how to construct a trifle, even making ice cream. The only task I was not allowed to do was lift things from the hob or the oven. Mum even allowed me to use her sharp knives.

Mum worked as soon as I went to school, so while I prepared the evening meal, she would do house work or vice versa. All the time there was thump, thump, thump, my brother kicking his football against the house wall. Dad repainted that every year, because the football made it so dirty.

Nick played football really well and dad thought he would one day play for Arsenal. He was also good at music, playing piano and guitar and he was in a pop band that had done a few little gigs, although the oldest of the group was only fourteen. Nick was just thirteen. Dad doted on Nick but didn't understand me at all. There was nothing in me that dad could identify with, because I was a boy but not his sort of boy. Had I the body of a girl, I suspect I would have been bounced on his knee, carried on his shoulders, caressed and cherished. The trouble was inside I might have been a girl but on the outside I was a boy but I didn't act like my father expected a boy and especially his son to act.

I heard mum and dad discussing me. It's surprising that parents fail to realise the acuteness of children's hearing. Dad described me as difficult. Mum replied that they had discussed this before and he knew what she thought. I didn't hear what she thought. Dad replied, 'Well you know my opinion on that. I think it's wrong and I sincerely hope you are wrong.'

I wondered what 'that' was. With all these undercurrents in the family, mainly caused by me, I was very unhappy. I didn't want to be the source of worry, nor the whipping boy. Sometimes I thought I was mad and thought I would end in a mad house, a looney-bin, although I had read so much stuff on the Net that should have convinced me to the contrary. I didn't understand the World I lived in. I felt like I had come from space, dumped here without any connections. I lacked the confidence to tell anyone how I really felt.

Consequently, mostly I felt a bit second-class and really I was. I mean I was great in school; my report was just covered in 'excellent' and even one 'impressive performance' comment from my teachers. In the behaviour column, I get 'caring and industrious but timorous'.

Trouble was, the brilliance I had for academia was as nothing compared to that of my brother in his extramural activities that might one day make him a fortune. Nick was outgoing, a boy everyone liked or was jealous of, a real boy but nice. He wasn't dim though his school report would give that impression, he just didn't have the energy or inclination for bookwork.

I liked my school, I loved learning, not just things like history which is just some long story of how we humans and particularly, we English arrived where we are today, but also maths and science and geography. Even French, though I don't think our teacher in junior school was very good. I just loved being educated, all subjects, well everything except kicking or hitting a ball with a stick. I spent hours finding out just anything. When I saw something I didn't know, I would look it up. My brother would let it wash by. If he didn't actually need to know, then it probably wasn't worth wasting time on it.

No, learning for the sake of knowing about the World was not for Nick. He hated Maths and English, French he said was a waste of time in fact everything that denied him time playing sport, was a waste of time and his report, except for sport was terrible. Dad used to tell him to try harder, but he was just one of those kids that muck about in class and only use their brains when they have a ball to hand or foot.

Chapter 3.   Saskia's Tale

I started writing this as a cathartic exercise. Now I'm writing this for Larry, for him to use as he thinks fit in his thesis.

Luckily my best friend lived at the bottom of our garden and we had a gate into theirs. Jenn and her parents were lovely to me. Jenn was just great and I went there to play her games. Mum said sometimes, 'Go and see your sweetheart,' you know joking like parents do, hoping to embarrass their kids, trying for some reaction. Why do they do that? I just find it, found it then, really annoying that a boy can't be a friend with a girl without sex raising its head. It's so stupid. It was very stupid, though mum didn't know it, because I thought of myself as a girl. I was Jenn's sister in my mind not her brother.

Whenever I felt too corralled at home, I would toddle off down the garden, under the two plum trees that gave such gorgeous fruit each September, and through the gate that gave access to their domain, the Jennings household. Never once was I turned away. If they were going out, Rebecca, Jenny's mum who is now my adoptive parent, would ring my mum and ask whether I could go with them. The answer was usually yes.

Rebecca seemed not to mind that I was girly, at least not boyish, in fact I think she quite liked it because Jenn and I got on so well together.

Like when we took a short break on the coast. We were on this caravan site and by chance, the people in the next van were acquaintances of mine, not them, not my brother who smirked and mocked, 'girly games'. Mary was a friend from school and the daughter of the village chemist and her friends. There was only my brother to play with other than the girls, and I was fed up being his henchman, holding his stupid kite that did nothing, or run after his glider or the tennis ball they used for French cricket. The girls were nice, it was light-hearted gentle fun and my family destroyed it.

I was just nine years old and I was playing the girls' games, like skipping and Queenie Queenie, and my parents had to comment and well, mock. It was hurtful and it made me self-conscious and spoiled my, our fun. So that next day when they knocked on our caravan door and asked if I was coming out to play I wouldn't. I still regret giving in to my family's prejudice.

Was it a wonder then that I drew into myself, and stopped telling them anything or spending much time with them? Playing with those girls was harmless fun, innocent fun. We were laughing happily together playing games that cost nothing, not even lost skin in a fall. Yet they had to make me feel self-conscious, a lesser person, a misfit.

Sometimes I hated mum and dad. I know I shouldn't have, but I'm trying to be really truthful in this account and I did hate them then for about a day and a half and my smirking brother too.

It seems the human race looks at other members of it and immediately, like sorting post, tries to stick one in a box. Proper boy, proper girl, gay, lesbian, tomboy, misfit, oddball. If you get one of the last five, they would believe anything of you. You are instantly dismissable by the straight people. Yet there is more criminality, more to fear amongst the 'normal' than amongst we deviants. I use the term deviant not to denigrate just to denote a departure from the norm.

So dear reader, you can see that even at that tender age of ten and a bit, I had been thinking about things and about my place in the World. I was terribly unhappy. That is why I was withdrawn, secretive, seeming without much humour, adrift from the rest of my family. Yet my parents did nothing to try to define the problem. They never said, 'Darling, tell us how you feel, what troubles you? It doesn't matter what it is we will do our best to help. Whatever you do we will support you. Dad was worst of all. I overheard his remarks about me time and again. What was really hurtful was my mum's half-hearted defence of me.

I was sort of like a fire, smouldering, a lot of heat beneath, wanting someone to blow the embers of thoughts and fears in my mind into open flame. They would then warm their hands on the blaze of my spirit and feed it, see the good in those flames, sound my heart and help. Instead as in the girly games, the little flame was mocked and snuffed. Was it any wonder, I turned inwards and went to Jenn and her mum, Mrs Jennings, Rebecca and spent so much time there?

Even now as I write, after eight years, I feel that bitterness, even after the awful tragedy that befell our family. I had thought with the passing of the last gloriously happy eight years, I had put all that behind me. Obviously the deep hurt of my eleventh year, still lingers.

Does one ever really get over the tragedies in ones life? Oh yes we survive just as I do. I swept all that happened in my eleventh year, the bad bits, into a bin and stacked that somewhere in the deep recesses of my mind like they do with nuclear waste. Nuclear waste of a nuclear family.

I have lived happily, very happily considering all my problems, for these last, well six years. It took me two years to recover from the events of that summer. Rebecca who became my mum was infinitely patient, drying my tears and rocking me. My new dad too. They knew the real me and my worth. It was their patience and love that brought me round.

Now I'm writing this, which I hope will be of interest to you and cathartic for me, in revisiting those times. Those old battles with my family and with my own self have surged to the surface and my old wounds have opened. Like any wound, I hope that opening it will allow any remaining poison to flow out.

Chapter 4.　　Saskia's Tale

I look out of my window onto the immaculate lawns and pruned trees of the inner courtyard of my beloved college. Students move about, keeping to the paths, stopping to chat, exchanging news and tips. A girl appears, blonde hair streaming behind from its capture in a hair band, lacrosse stick in hand and she waves to me and heads for her room across the lawn. My beloved Jenny, my adopted sister. We came up together, by an absolute fluke I think or perhaps a board with some humanity, settling us in the same college. We wave at each other from across the lawn and make signals to go eat or have a drink or coffee. Yes I love that girl, my darling sister Jenn.

Now I have to lay down just how it was that Jenn became my sister and her parents adopted me. Well, I think I will stop for the moment. I need to think about this, sort things in my mind. I have to really go back these eight years and remember everything.

Oh those dark horrible days of that glorious summer, when the days seemed to dawn sunny for weeks. I'm going down to the velodrome to ride the bike round and round, just me against the clock. I'll have some coaching if a coach is there, push my muscles and will to win to the limit and while I follow the monotony of the oval track, try to think things through.

When people say 'it's not fair' or 'they don't deserve that' when bad luck befalls, I always shudder. There is no law that says life has to be fair. It is a lottery from conception to death. A split second, an innocent decision can alter ones life forever. Does anyone deserve to be blown up by a terrorist bomb or struck by lightening? Does anyone deserve to be born with limbs that don't work? Of course not.

When someone obviously talented has a misfortune, people like to make it a worse tragedy. It's the same for anyone. Yes the rich are able to deal with misfortune better than the poor, of course, but the personal hardship is the same.

When Nick died it was just terrible. I was at school. Dad was on the rig at the time so it was left to mum to manage us kids. Nick got this headache and mum thought at first he was just throwing a sickie. Then she felt his forehead and that was it, he was off to the doctor. The GP said Nick had a virus. Of course it wasn't just a virus. It was meningitis. Three hours after first seeing the GP he was on the way to hospital, mum driving him to hospital apparently like a mad thing. I was at school.

They tried everything and they told mum they were going to amputate his legs and some fingers. We, I was staying with Jenn, were horrified. Mum phoned dad and he was getting the next helicopter off the rig. There were tears all round. I mean if any kid ever wanted legs, it was my brother. I hardly knew what was going on because being the youngest and well just being me, quiet, mum says withdrawn, I just didn't seem to count. I found out what's happening just by listening to one-sided conversations on the telephone and fitted it all together like a puzzle, filling in the gaps. It's as though I wasn't a real family member, they didn't want me to know. I found out by listening.

Some of this I only know because Rebecca has told me about it. Just before the operation was due to begin, Nick died. He was actually in the lift to the operating theatres. They tried resuss but he was in such a bad state by then, they couldn't revive him. It was terrible. Mum was really brave for at least a day and then collapsed. Dad was flown home. He was devastated. Poor Dad. All his dreams were shattered as well as losing his beloved son. It was like the end of the World. No kid likes to see parents cry, and they tried not to in front of me, but I could hear it from afar, from my bedroom, I would here the tortured conversation, the strangulated voices and with that, the bad temper. Almost worse were the long silences as though our house itself had turned into a grave. I stayed with Jenn for five nights.

The next weeks were horrible. I kept out of the way more than usual. Thank goodness for Rebecca who gave me a spare bedroom. It was as though Nick had been the cement between Mum and Dad, the only thing they had in common. Oh dad was OK to me, I mean it was all Nick but he was never horrid, well once he called me Sissy Boy to my face, but apart from that. No there were other times too now I think back.

There was never that warmth I experienced in Jenn's home not even really from Mum. Even Jenn's dad liked me and played little jokes on me, like taking fifty pence pieces from behind my ear and giving them to me. And he would cuddle Jenn and me at the same time when he came home.

When Nick was alive, it was, 'Come on I'll bowl to you,' in our garden or at the seaside, beach cricket, dad would round up any kids who were doing nothing and get a game going. Of course even I would join in then but it would be a fluke if I survived an over, and bowling, dad said he'd seen girls bowl better. He didn't mean to be cruel, but it was cruel. It was destroying me little by little and as they say now, alienating me from the family.

What I really needed was encouragement, some coaching because I lacked Nick's natural ability. I gave up on sport completely, so of course they went to events without me.

Those days after Nick died, I hope were the worst days of my life. The rows between Mum and Dad became more frequent. Even pots were thrown in the kitchen. They were both in a mess; we were all in a mess. I 'spose I recovered soonest, I mean he was only my brother but he had been the apple of Dad's eye and of course mums always have that tie with their children and especially the first born. But it was Nick who had been the cement between the two of them.

After Nick's funeral, dad went back to the rig, glad I think to be away from all the associations that reminded him of his golden boy. It was a silent house, just mum and me. Nick had provided life, vibrancy. He had been noisy and boisterous. You always knew when Nick was in the house, there was piano playing or his electric guitar or his radio or he was playing with a ball against the wall. That bang, bang bang of the ball, may have been annoying but it was like a heartbeat. After his death, it was horrible.

When he'd gone it was like being in a Cathedral. Everyone seemed to be tiptoeing around, whispering rather than talking as though any noise would upset Nick's ghost and then Nick would really be gone forever. I even found dad crying. He was in the garden, digging the vegetable patch and I went up to be with him, to try to get him to like me just a bit and saw the tears running down his face.

'Dad, you're crying.'

'Don't be daft, it's sweat,' he said, but it wasn't. His voice didn't sound right either, all tight and that could have been caused by the effort of digging but it wasn't. Dad was a very fit man. I wanted to hug him but we weren't a touchy feely family. I knew dad didn't like me, even though I was then his only child. It's a terrible realisation when one admits someone dislikes you, even worse when one knows a parent despises you. I heard too many whispers.

I wanted to be hugged. Oh how I wished to be hugged as my best friend at the bottom of our garden, Jenny was hugged and caressed. I knew she was an only child so Jenny was extra special to them, doubly so because her mum had another but it was stillborn. She couldn't have more, so Jenn was very precious. Her parents hugged each other and Jenn. Her mum and dad even hugged me. At home, I got no hugs.

I was on a half day, home from school at lunch. I told mum about dad being in tears. 'Oh,' she said as though she was exasperated. 'You better get yourself ready for the dentist this afternoon,' she said quite crossly.

I should explain, I'm having my teeth straightened, that wire thing on them pulling them into line and making sure I don't resemble a Derby winner. Dental visits are frequent.

So we go in mum's car the five miles to town and we sit there silent in the waiting room. I read National Geographic, full of articles about wildlife, discovery and peoples of far off lands. I'm called in twenty minutes late and he removes the wire thing and does something and then it's replaced. I hate the thing but if I don't want to look like a horse, and I don't, I just have to put up with it. I want nice teeth.

We do shopping at the big supermarket on the way home. I push the trolley and I try to be helpful. Mum's not in a good mood, she's not receptive to my helpful ideas or hints about ice cream or the honey breakfast flakes. I bump the trolley in the fruit section and mum tears me off a strip. I get the hint and shut up. We do it all in silence after that. She bumps into Mrs Knapton and they gossip, about Nick and I see mum nearly in tears and then they embrace and, oh God, this is all so dreadful. Their life is shit and so is mine.

I run out of the shop into the fresh air and sit on the shop windowsill and howl. I can't cope either. My home is devastated. Yes I always had my problems but six weeks ago it was a place full of love, at least between mum dad and Nick, now it's a place almost bereft of life. My parents seem to hate each other. They have no time for me and won't allow me to comfort them at all and all the time, I'm grieving too. Over the last few months, helping Nick understand maths and

English, we children had become closer. Nick was quite nice to me. I want to shout at them, 'I'm grieving too and I'm still here.'

OK, Nick and I didn't always get on that much but we were there for each other, as much as two kids who have almost nothing in common except blood can be.

A woman stops and asks if I'm all right and I nod and say yes. There's doubt in her expression but after hesitating, she moves away. Mum exits, pushing the laden trolley.

'Thank you for helping me Edward, just when I need you, you disappear.' She chides me. As though I don't feel bad enough already. I start to cry. I can't help it. My World was shaken off its axis by Nick's death, and what's left of it is being destroyed by their grief. This day eight weeks after the funeral is turning out to be the worst ever.

Mum stops and she grabs me and gives me a shake and then hugs me so tightly I can hardly breathe. 'I'm sorry I know it's hard for you too.' She says and kisses my head.

I walk, one hand on the trolley as though I need that to guide me, my eyes filled and my breathing in gasps. I let out a whine. We put the groceries in the boot and I take the trolley to the park.

I return to the car. I'm still crying. Mum hands me a man size, 'Dry your eyes and blow your nose. You feel so deeply don't you. I love you Edward. I'm sorry I don't always show it.'

Chapter 5.   Saskia's Tale

Over the next week, mum and dad are rowing or silent. Either way, I find it really dreadful. When they row, I run to Jenn's, through the gate and bang on their door and hope they will give me sanctuary. Sometimes I arrive in tears and Rebecca, Jenn's mum pulls me in and hugs me. My face aches from crying, my head hurts. I don't want to go on living if this is how life is to be. Dad is home all this week and I feel it would be better if he wasn't. He is absolutely heartbroken. He does nothing while mum, as mums do, carries on with the essentials of cooking and cleaning and looking after us. I know she is hurting too. I catch her at the stove choking back her tears. It's awful. Parents aren't meant to cry at least not in front of their children.

Then there comes a day that I hope is never repeated. It's over three weeks later and instead of matters easing, they are worse. The row starts at breakfast, I don't know what over, perhaps it was an overflow from the night before. They are both angry and I feel my world is coming to an end. I'm nervous and upset, I hate arguments, hate hearing grown ups, especially my parents arguing and backbiting like a pack of wolves I saw on TV. Their quarrels are destroying me. I pick up the sugar pot for my porridge and it slips and I drop it onto the table and it spills.

Dad yells, 'You stupid little Sissy, you can't catch and you can't even handle a sugar bowl. Why wasn't it you?'

He doesn't need to say what *it* is. I know. Why wasn't it me that died he means. I started to howl and mum hits him with the wooden spoon from the porridge, hard on his wrist.

'You,' he says, 'your negligence allowed him to die.'

Mum's face is white, even her lips.

I run from the room and a furious row commences. I run up to my bedroom and dive under my duvet, hands over my ears. I can't bear it.

There's silence. And I take my hands from my ears and listen. I emerge from the duvet. I hear the back door bang and see dad walk up the garden. He picks up the spade and starts to turn over his vegetable patch, violent, powerful thrusts of the spade into the soil.

Mum comes up the stairs. 'Where are you Edward?'

I don't speak. I just go to the door.

'There you are.'

'Mum,' I say.

I howl. I'm so miserable I wish it was me had died.

'Yes Edward. It's not your fault. Come on we're going out. There's an early film at the cinema followed by a bit of shopping.'

We go down and more or less straight out to the car. We go to the Mall where we can park for free as long as we buy cinema tickets. Mum parks and we make our way up to the cinema by escalators. There's a choice of films, Star Wars or the Secret of Moonacre about a girl orphan. I choose that.

'You would choose the girl film of course. Still rather that than Star Wars.'

I love the film and at least it's a relief, an escape from our troubles at home.

After we emerge from the dark into the dim foyer and then into the strong light of day. We walk the Mall. She keeps looking in jewellers' windows. Eventually she enters a shop and speaks to the assistant who produces a tray of gold chains and mum chooses one and then together we look at gold lockets and we choose one together, Mum writes something on a card and asks for the locket to be engraved. She pays and asks that they mail it to us when it's ready. From there we go to the supermarket and buy food for the week.

Mum drives home and I'm dreading walking in the door. Dad hates me. He wished me dead. The film had been light relief for two hours, holding mum's hand and crying at the film rather than my own life.

If I thought it the worst day ever, it really is. When we get home, dad's not there. The fork and wheelbarrow stand where he was working in the garden. His car is gone from the drive.

'Where the hell has he gone?' mum says, not so much a question, just a statement of annoyance. I say nothing. I can't say anything because I don't know what to say.

'Help me carry things in,' she says as though I wasn't going to. Of course I was, that's what I do. Nick played ball, I'm the swot and the one that helps around the place and yet, Nick was always the favourite or so it seemed to me. I grab two bags and march in through the front door. I take the shopping through to the kitchen and return just as mum is shutting the door, struggling with three more bags. I pick two up and carry them through.

I start to put things away, the frozen and cold foods first in the fridge and freezer. That done the other stuff goes in the pantry, bringing the old to the front and the new behind. Mum has disappeared and I feel like the maid, left to do all the chores and while I don't mind doing stuff around the place, even dusting and vacuuming, it's nice to be appreciated and it's nice to do it with my mum.

I put the empty shoppers near the door to be stored in the car boot for next time and after that I look for mum to tell her it's all stowed. She's not anywhere downstairs. I go up and look in the bathroom then my parents en suite. Finally I go to their bedroom and look through the crack between door and the jamb and see mum sitting on the bed. I enter silently and she is sitting rocking, back and forth and I know she is crying. It's unbearable. I feel like I don't want to go on living if this is what life is going to be.

Somehow, though I have never seen this before, I know she's in distress and I walk around the bed and sitting beside her, I put an arm around her. There are tears, real tears running down her cheeks and the silent sobs suddenly become a shriek, a howl of pain and I fling my arms around her. I thought the worst moment of my life was when I heard Nick had died on the way to the operating theatre. This is worse, my mum howling like a wounded animal, making a sound I have never before experienced. No child should ever hear a parent howl like that. It sounded like the end of the World as I imagined the end of the World would appear, after that man on the doorstep showed us a picture of people being consumed by fire and told us the end of the World is nigh, when all souls that were not saved would suffer in hell. I had bad dreams for a week after that. Mum's howl was worse.

'Mum don't. Please mum, don't.'

She pulled me in and I thought she would crush me. At least she stopped howling and I stopped crying. We just hugged, two miserable humans unable to cope with what life had thrown our way. Gradually she ceased and I ceased. She felt cold; her hand on my hand was cold.

How long we sat on her bed I don't know, but my legs were dangling down and going to sleep because the blood was cut off.

Because I know I'll have to get up I say, 'Mum, what's happened now.'

'Your father's left us a letter.'

'What do you mean mum?'

'He's gone away.'

'But he'll be back for tea tonight?'

'He's not coming back. He's left us.'

I'm stunned. Why I want to ask but I can't. I feel this is so wrong. We sit there on her bed, her dressing table just a few feet away and I see all her things left there, hair brush and comb, five different bottles of perfume that make her smell so sweet, a little silver dish she puts her everyday jewellery in. I love the smell of her room, a mixture of the perfumes she uses, a feminine room. Her vanity and the drawers where she keeps her very best, most feminine undies, the ones I covet so much.

'I put everything away mum. Mum why has he left us?'

'He's heartbroken over Nick.'

'But he's still got us.'

'It's not enough seemingly.'

'What will we do mum?'

'I don't know Edward, I just don't know. Maybe when he's had a few days, he'll come back. I don't care anymore.'

I say nothing. Not caring is the worst thing. She has to care, care for herself and care for me. We sit for about another ten minutes. Mum sort of recovers and says in a voice almost normal.

'Edward, why don't you see if Jenny is next door and go there while I tidy up?'

'I want to stay here mum and help.'

'You're a good child. Edward, I know you're unhappy. I think I know why. The film choice confirmed it. You would rather be a girl, I think that's right isn't it? You can say now dad's not here. Don't be afraid, you can tell me.'

'Mum I....' I was going to lie. Then I think, my life cannot be worse and she doesn't sound cross. I should tell the truth for a change. 'Yes mum, from always, from before I knew about boys and girls bits.'

'My poor child. We'll have to make that happen then.'

'Really mum? Mum, are you all right if I go to Jenn's?'

'I'm all right. Go and play with Jenny, there's a dear, please. I have letters to write. I want you to be happy. Remember that.'

'Yes mum.'

'Run along then.'

'OK mum.'

So I leave and walk down the stairs, listening although I don't want to, for sounds of her grief. The house is silent, so silent as it never was when my brother was alive. It's horrible.

I leave by the back door and walk up our garden that runs parallel to the road and through the gate into Jenny's. I knock the door.

Jenny's mum, Rebecca or as I call her Mrs Jennings answers the door.

'Hello Edward. Come in. Jenny's upstairs in her bedroom. You know the way. Your mum just rang me so I'm going to see her.'

'Oh. That's why she sent me to play with Jenn. Thank you Mrs Jennings.' I go up the stairs and along the landing to the door at the end that says, 'Private, Keep Out'. Jenny is the same age as me, nearly, just a couple of months older. I knock her door.

'Come in Edward.' She has ears that could hear a pin drop at twenty metres.

I push through the door into her room. It's quite a large room with a big wardrobe and she has everything there, her desk and her computer and it's pretty, nice curtains and also net curtains, not across but hanging for effect like the window has a lace petticoat under the curtains. She has dolls and teddy bears, no other animals except for a panda that I think is a sort of bear anyway.

She swims; I mean swims in what they call galas. Why are they called that? What's wrong with match? There are photos of swimming and a couple of I suppose Olympic stars holding their gold medals but I have never heard of them.

She has clothes all over in neat piles except for some thrown on the floor.

'What's up?' She asks.

'It's just awful. Dad's left. We went shopping and when mum and I came home, he'd gone, left a note. He's just heartbroken because of Nick and I think mum and dad weren't really getting on. Mum's crying. She asked me to come and see you.' Oh God help me, I started to cry too.

I sat on her bed and screwed up my eyes and panted trying to subdue my sobs. Jenny threw her arms around me and kissed my cheek. She produced a paper hankie and mopped my tears.

'Look I'm sorting my tops into colours, everything is colour coordinated. Do you want to do that while I go down and get us some drinks? Won't be a min.'

She disappeared leaving me with her tops. I knelt on the floor leaving the bed as a platform to place the tops. I started with pink and moved to cream, then white a blue and what mum always describes as eau de Nil. She had a dress that colour almost but more blue.

Jenny reappeared with the drinks. 'Mum's gone to see your mum. Oh you've done well. Put them on these hangers then I can put them in the wardrobe, oh but not that one, it's going in the charity shop.'

I picked up the little blouse with puff sleeves and the matching pearl buttons. 'It's really pretty. You have such pretty clothes. You're so lucky being a girl. Mum just asked if I wanted to be a girl, if that was why I'm so quiet and sad?'

'And? What did you say?'

'Always.'

'Why? I'm just a girl; you're just a boy. That's how we are, isn't it.'

'Yes that's how we are, physically. In my brain, I'm a girl. Nick was such a boy in every way. Dad really loved him, he blames mum for Nick's death. Now Dad's gone away and I don't know whether he will ever come back. Dad never loved me like he did Nick.'

'What about your mum? She loves you as much?'

'I don't think so.'

'Has she said so?'

'No but, I just feel I haven't come up to scratch, not boyish enough. I'm studious......'

'But a bit girly!'

'That's what Nick always said, you're so girly. All of them. And I am. I'm proud of being girly because I think I have a girl brain. I can't help being who I am. I can't be Nick but I'm me, clever me top of the class and so unhappy.' I start to cry again.

Jenny flings her arms around me. Again. She smells sweet. She keeps one hand on each of my shoulders and looks into my face. 'Do you want me to tell the truth or to butter you?'

'What truth?'

'What I really think, what mum and me think.'

'About what?'

'About you silly.'

'You don't like me either then?'

'Did I say that? Are you strong enough, with all this going on, your family and that? Perhaps now's the wrong time.'

'No now you started you better say otherwise I shall just worry. Go on then, what do you think.' I looked at her through eyes still filled with tears. 'I'm a loser, go on say it.'

'No you're not. You are clever clogs. You must never lose that. Me and mum have talked about you. We think you should have been a girl. Mum said to dad, 'That poor boy, put him in a dress and no one would think he wasn't a girl.'

'I can't help my looks!' I say defensively and a little huffily.

'Shhh. Don't be upset. It's not that, not just that. It's the way you do things. You skip about, boys don't. You always greet people with your lovely open smile, boys don't. You like holding hands, I've seen you with my mum and yours feeling for a hand. The way you move and you can't catch for toffee, I've seen you. Worst of all perhaps your hands, the way you use them wide open not half closed. Mum and I talked about it a lot after we came back from that picnic, before Nick died. She said you're graceful and she caught you pirouetting in your garden when she popped round to see your mum.'

I sat down on the bed and I bent double, head almost on my knees. I was so miserable and these remarks were doing nothing to cheer me. She sat beside me and put an arm around me.

'Doesn't mean we don't like you. We do, I do. If I could have a brother or sister I would have you. We've always been friends, right from tots. You've been the brother I never had. I don't mind that you are more like a sister. I got the best of both worlds.'

'That's what you think of me?'

'Fraid so!'

'Golly. No wonder dad never hardly gave me the time of day and mum's sometimes so impatient. See, I was right. I'm just no use.'

'Not a lot of use as a boy, it's true but you'd make a lovely girl.'

'I'm not pretty enough.'

'Oh yes you are. You're very pretty, don't you realise?'

'I just look like a girly boy.'

'That's what you see. We don't see that. We see a girl in boy clothes.'

Chapter 6.　　　Saskia's Tale

An ambulance siren comes nearer and nearer and finally stops not far away, the siren appears to choke, ending in a squeal. A door slams and Jenn jumps up to look out of the window.

'Nothing. Don't know where that is. So where were we? Oh yes, I know and you said no wonder your dad thought you were no use.'

'No I said I was no use.'

'Ed that's a dreadful thing to say about yourself.'

'It's true. I know I'm girly, that's why the kids take the pee. I can't make myself like Nick was. Everyone loved him. Me I'm nothing.'

'You are who you are. You're my best friend, you always will be. Doesn't that count for something?'

'Of course. You're my best friend too. I don't know what I'd have done without you.'

She was looking at me a slight smile playing about her mouth. She reached out and brushed my hair with her fingers. 'You have lovely hair, so sleek and it looks like quite dark but when the light gets in it there's all sorts going on, blond and red and brown and it sparkles and shines. Are you growing it?'

I blushed. Is it boyish to grow ones hair? 'I....well sort of. I just didn't want it cut.'

She turned to her vanity and opened a small top drawer. She turned back to me, with a hair slide in her teeth. She used her brush and brushed my hair. I made no protest, I liked it, loved her, the sister I had wanted and never had.

She brushed my hair this way and that. Finally she put the hair slide in. Something happened within me. A thrill. Just that small action, some brushing of my hair and a slide, like a girl and suddenly I was filled with joy and I realised with a jolt, an understanding of myself that had not been there before, not as strong as it now was. Yes of course I always knew what attracted me, but this action playing with my best friend, just reinforced that feeling. I felt desperate but excited.

'Shoot. I see what they mean. Have a look in the mirror.'

I looked and this alien creature looked back at me, more female than male.

'What?' I asked her pretending I couldn't see the girl there. 'So it's just me with a hair slide.'

'Don't you see?' Then she laughed. 'Ah you're pretending aren't you, cos to admit what you see would be embarrassing. OK. You coy thing, I won't say boy. I dare you. Wear what I give you. You have to promise me here and now, you don't back out. If you agree, you are in my power and you have to do what I say.'

The very idea of being in her power in this way was a thrill. Why did I feel this way? Was this the way a boy behaved, liking being in someone's power, obeying someone else's will. In a moment of ecstasy and reckless abandon I said, 'OK.'

'Strip down to your knickers.'

'Pants.'

'Pants, knickers, panties. Go on you promised.'

'I won't take them off.'

'Did I tell you to? I'm waiting. Obey me.' And she made motions with her hands as if casting a spell. I stripped feeling rather stupid.

She rummaged in her wardrobe and I heard hangers moving across the rail. From behind the door she said, 'Ah the very one.'

She produced a frock or should I say dress, I never know, granny always spoke about frocks and mum dresses. This dress whatever, was a delicate pink with quite a full skirt, short sleeves, like elbow length and a little white collar and V neck. Christ I sound like a girl just describing it but then it's not the first time I've looked at dresses, often pouring over my mum's Next catalogue when I had a private moment.

'You like?'

'It's lovely. Your Christmas dress. Really you want me to wear that?'

'Do you dare?'

I blushed I could feel the blood rise into my damned face. When that happened I usually got really confused and wanted to run. I wouldn't this time.

'I dare if you help me.' She was already undoing buttons with dextrous girl fingers, and then she was slipping it over my head and doing up the shirt waister top and straightening. She eyed me critically. 'Now drop your pants, just reach under the skirt like this and pull them down and put these on.' She held out some pink girl pants. 'Go on, you promised.' I did as she commanded.

She watched. She giggled. 'Oh my god, Edwina, you're so pretty, that colour really suits. Here look at Edwina.' She pulled me to look in her full-length mirror.

'Well?'

'OMG. I'm a girl.'

'You are indeed. Edwina. I don't like that name though even if I did think of it.' She tilted her head on one side. 'Mmm. I know, Saskia. That's what I'm calling you. My sister Saskia, golly that sounds so nice. Do you like it? Saskia. Oh Saskia, yes she's going out with Richard. Yes they are thinking of getting engaged. She's so pretty, my best friend, well more like a sister really, Saskia. My sister, that's what I call her though she isn't really, not by blood, but as I made her, yes she is mine.'

We heard the back door bang and then footsteps on the stairs. Her mum put her head round the door.

'Oh here you are. Edward, your mum says you can spend the night here. The spare bed is all made up. Your mum's gone out to see someone. Is that OK?'

'Who?' I ask, feeling further shut out at getting a message from mum indirectly.

'Oh just people, about your dad leaving so sudden. That dress looks really nice on you.'

I blush a deeper pink than the dress. Should that compliment please me so much?

'Jenny I have an errand to run and I'll be back as soon as. Look after our guest won't you!'

'Course I will mum.'

'And you are on no account to leave the house Jenny, either of you. Now I'm trusting you both?'

'Mum of course.'

'Your father is going to be home later but not until about nine or ten, he's in Liverpool and it's a dreadful journey.'

'We'll get our tea then mum. What shall I do?'

'Salad, you can do that and there's ham or smoked salmon in the fridge. Leave some for me. And put one of those French sticks in the oven, you know how to do them don't you. Two of them as we have a guest.'

'Yes mum. We're just having a chat, then we'll do it.'

'Good girls, kids. You don't leave the house, either of you. Is that understood?'

'Yes mum, we said.'

'Good.'

She disappeared her footsteps receding down the stairs and the front door slammed.

There was the sound of a car starting and wheels crunching on gravel. Jenn looked out of the window. 'Just mum running her errand, she always flying about. I expect she's off to the supermarket.'

'You are such a tease and it's been fun now I should get back to being miserable me.'

'No you are still in my power. How do you feel? Look at yourself again. That's you, that gorgeous girl in the mirror. I know you like what you see. Mum and I always said you are more girl than boy. You are aren't you? Isn't that what you have always thought? You once said when we were about seven, you wished you were a girl. Now you are. Well I know you have boy bits, but I bet we could go out, even though your hair is not that girly yet and you would pass.'

I was turning in front of the mirror and feeling the skirt against my legs and the slight rush of air as I turned this way and that. It rustled delightfully. I burst into tears.

'Oh god I'm sorry. I've upset you. Get it off.'

I sat on the bed and rocked, just like mum was this afternoon when she found Dad had left us. Jenny was hugging me again and gave me a wet kiss on the cheek. 'I'm so sorry.' She said again. 'That's the last thing I wanted, to upset you on this day, when your dad has left and all. Please don't tell mum, she'll be so angry with me.'

'No nnnot you, not what you've done, well it is,' I sobbed. 'It's just how I've always wanted to be, a girl in a dress. It's like some lovely dream and yet I know the reality is, I'm a boy and I'm having all these sissy thoughts and I hate myself because I'm not the boy Nick was and that's why my parents don't love me and that's why although I'm clever I'll never be any good. That's why dad has left and why mum is so upset and it's because I'm not a proper boy. I'm nothing.'

'Hey that's not true. You are the clever one. Look Nick was a handsome boy and he was good at sports. Say he had made it as a top soccer star, he would have made it until what thirty, then what, downhill, playing for lesser clubs and then maybe nothing, they don't all live happily ever after. You are what you are, mum said that when we were talking about you. She said I had to accept you for what you are and that's a person I love like you were my brother.... Huh yes even if you are my sister. I see you there, even with tears and see you in that dress and a bit more girly hairstyle and I love you as my sister. Here, look let me slip this on your wrist.' She slipped a silver bangle over my hand. 'And shoes, come on, let's finish you. Here these little pumps. Can you get them on?'

She was on her knees fitting the pumps to my un-protesting body. 'There! Is this how you wanted to be? It is isn't it from what you said and watching your face as I changed you. Saskia? It is isn't it?'

I nodded in shame knowing boys aren't supposed to like dresses and bracelets and fussing with hair. 'I'm so ashamed.'

'You shouldn't be. What do they say, the gays? 'Out and proud'. Mum says you can't be what you're not. She said that about you. Do you want to change back into boy things? I don't think so. You like being girly, you are girly. You just have to lose that boy pride. That's what Dad said. He knew too. I'm going to plait your hair. One or two?'

She bunched my hair. 'I think two. You'll have to grow it more or have a bob. Anyway I plait it for now.'

Expertly she divided my hair and plaited one side and then the other, fastening them with elastic and then ribbons near enough the colour of the dress.

'Now see.'

I looked in the mirror. 'Wow, Jenny! I love it.'

I knew as I boy, I should strip the dress off and laugh and throw it in her face. I didn't. I nodded. I try to be nonchalant isn't that the word?

'I don't mind what you put me in. It doesn't matter.' Of course it did, it mattered so much.

'Saskia!'

Even calling me that thrilled me. Saskia. How I loved the name.

'Downstairs, we have to get tea make the salad and put the bread in the oven, so when mum gets back it's ready.'

'What like this? In your beautiful dress?'

'Why not? It's just clothes and you already said you like it. Mum always said, that boy, meaning you, is more girl than boy, so what's to stop you.' Even then she was leading me to the door. 'Besides mum has already seen you. She said you looked nice and you do.'

We descended to the kitchen and I loved being Saskia. It was as though my half-life had ended, I had escaped the shell that surrounded me and here I was out at last, a young chick proud of my new feathers and somehow as we worked I became even more girly, I caught myself swirling around the table with my hips and wearing the apron my friend or my sister had made me tie about my waist after

119

slipping it over my head. We put the bread in the oven and turned the oven up a bit higher as we were a little late. We kept looking in between making the salad. The bread looked done, it was turning golden brown but when we took it out it looked more pale, so we bashed it back in and chatted and then after five minutes took it out and it might have been a bit over but when we tore one apart, it was fine, nice and crusty and soft inside. We were just ready when we heard the door and Mrs Jennings came into the kitchen.

I wanted to hide but Jenny held tight to my hand.

'Well you have been busy. Everything ready?'

'Yes mum.'

'Then let's eat.'

She seemed not to even notice that I was now a girl, well outwardly.

She took drinks from the fridge and fetched glasses from the cupboard and then a few extra condiments from the cupboard. We ate in comparative silence, Mrs Jennings just talking about the weekend and the things they had to do, Jenny's ballet lesson first thing Saturday, first on the list.

'Ed you are going to be with us for the weekend because your mum is busy. Why don't you go to ballet? We can lend you something, don't look frightened, not a tutu not yet, but some ballet shoes if you can get them on and tights and shorts. What do you say?'

'Oh say yes Saskia,' Jenny said. 'Don't be shy. Come with me.'

'But I don't know anything about ballet. I'd look a fool.'

'They all start sometime. There's other boys there if that's what's worrying you.'

'He wants to be a girl mum. We always knew didn't we. We discussed, the wrong body thing like Jazz on TLC.'

'Hush now Jenny. Don't bully. Let's eat and Ed or Saskia can think about it.'

So we ate the salad and the bread dripping with olive oil and balsamic vinegar and the ham and our salad and it was lovely. After we cleared, we went into the sitting room.

'Come and sit by me.' She commanded. Dutifully I did as I was told. 'Smooth that skirt out as you sit so it doesn't crease. Go on, you know how, I've seen you studying Jenny all these years. That's it. So what's going on with you, not your family, that's for later. No Jenny, you don't speak. Why have you allowed her to dress you like this.'

She fingered my pig tails. 'You look authentic.'

I blushed and didn't know what to say. Then she reached and pulled me to her so I was cuddled into her side and it was the most delicious feeling, the most love I'd felt in a long time. She bent her head and kissed the top of my head, I felt her hot breath right through my hair.

'Come on, you are among friends here, more than that. Jenny loves you and so do I. Now deep breath. Go.'

'I always wanted to be a girl. I think of myself as a girl but I do know I'm not, I mean I have a boy body and if I stay like this, then I'll become a man and……and that's just about the worst thing I can think of, being a man. Not that there's anything wrong with being a man, just that, not for me. I just hate being a boy.' I've said it quickly, let it gush out before my nerves get the better of me and make me clam up.

'So what Jenny has done, turning you into Saskia, that's how you'd like to be?'

'Yes.'

'You say always? How long?'

'Ages, since ever I can remember.'

'All those years?'

'Yes.' And then I start to cry.

'Hey now! Shush darling. I'm not cross, not at all. If you want to be Saskia while you stay with us, that's all right, really we all think you're a girl anyway, don't we Jenny?'

'Even daddy, well him most of all.'

'So now, look your mum has had to go away for a bit, she's sad because of your brother dying and then your dad leaving. So you are here with us. I dare say we can let you be Saskia as long as that's not going to muddle you up. You know you're a boy don't you?'

'Yes.'

'But you feel like a girl, you feel like Saskia?'

'Yes.'

'It's just you have the wrong body, isn't that it?'

'Yes that's it. I've always thought of myself as a girl and I hated being a boy and having boy stuff, clothes and toys and being made to feel I was wrong because I wasn't like Nick. He was a boy. I'm just not.'

'No you're certainly not. Then Saskia you shall be. Well it's time for bed. Up stairs the pair of you, the spare room's all ready.'

'Mum can't she sleep with me mum?'

'Well I don't know.'

'Mum my bed's a double, we can easily fit in.'

'Well all right but you behave yourselves, no naughtiness. You can find Saskia a nighty. Up you go to the bathroom Saskia. Into the shower with you, there's a shower cap in the bathroom if you don't want to wet that hair. Good wash mind and brush your teeth. I'll get you your own brush head for the electric toothbrush. It will be the purple band for you, Jenny has pink.'

I wash and I'm soon dry and I put the nighty on and clean knickers too, all laid out for me by Jenny. And it's so good, I almost forget about dad leaving. I'm wondering what mum's doing as I lie in bed, waiting for Jenny.

Jenny comes in in her nighty and bounces into bed followed by her mum.

'I know you usually have a story but it's late and I'm tired, so not tonight girls. Sleep tight. Go to sleep. I'll find you something to wear in the morning Saskia.'

She kissed us both.

'Night mum, I love you.' Jenny says.

I take my cue from that. 'Good night Mrs Jennings.' I, can I say it, 'I love you.'

'Bless you. Love you Jenny, love you Saskia.'

We cuddle up and Jenny talks and I'm asleep in no time.

Chapter 4.

I woke finding myself in strange surroundings and realised quickly that I was in Jenny's bedroom, quite safe and sound. I'm wearing a nighty and last night when I went to bed I was Saskia. That memory and those thoughts made me all warm inside. I felt the nighty and because it was wrapped around my middle, I untangled it and pulled it down over my legs. I lay there thinking, thinking about Nick and dad and wondered what mum was doing. What would mum say to Saskia? Would I still be Saskia? It was dreadful if the freedom I felt now would later be denied.

A hand grasped my shoulder.

'Hello Saskia,' followed by a chuckle.

I turned and looked into the face of my very best friend Jenny Jennings.

'How are you? Did you sleep OK?'

'Mmm like a top. It's a good bed. This is the first time I've ever slept with someone else.'

'First here too. And are you still Saskia?'

'If I can be. Your mum was great, I mean really great, lovely. At first I thought she was cross then I don't know, like she softened.'

'She was worried, she said something about opening Pandora's box whatever that is, but it's something like letting out a secret and then it can never be a secret again. She could see how happy you were although you were shy about it. I heard dad come home and I went out to the loo and I could hear them talking and talking. They must have been talking half the night. Anyway, we best get up. Do you want to shower or are you clean? I'll not shower but I might after ballet. You are going to do ballet?'

'I said I would. Will they laugh at me?'

'Course not. There is something. I think you need to sort out whether you're going to be Ed or Saskia there. Whether you're a ballerina or a danseur. A girl dancer or a boy because it's different, not just points but other things, like boys, we call them danseurs, do huge leaps and lifts and we have to hold more positions and spins, which are called pirouettes.'

'Will I be able to, I'm not very coordinated.'

'Not straight off, that's what the training is all about.'

'Then it's ballerina of course.'

'Then you wear a tutu. That will be fun, It's just a little elasticated waist skirt.'

'Fine.'

'Fine?'

'Yes, I always wanted one.'

'I always knew you were girly but not how much of a girl. You must have been in agony seeing me with my dresses and girl stuff. Poor you. I have been torturing you all these years without meaning to.'

'Well yes, of course it's been torture seeing you with girl stuff and doing girl things but you didn't mean to torture me. My life was just so rubbish. In any case, I spent so much time here doing girl stuff, that made life bearable.'

'Why didn't you come out and tell your mum and dad?'

'Because, well, I already didn't measure up against Nick and I just thought that would be the end, they would, I don't know, hate me. I did tell my mum this afternoon at the supermarket.'

'What did she say?'

'She said she loves me, always had. She wished she'd shown it more.'

'Poor you, thinking your parents hate you.'

'I'm just hoping your mum will talk them into understanding me. It's the wrong time I know, just after Nick's gone, and dad now deserted us, but would there ever be a good time? I'm much happier now someone knows, like you and your mum. She's great your mum, nothing seems to phase her.'

'No but she has been sad too. After me there was another baby but it was still born and now mum can't have any more kids. That's why it's just me and now you, well you some of the time.'

'I love being here with you Jenn.'

'Good I should hope so, after all we are Besties. OK getting up. I'll find you something to wear. You'll have to get your own clothes, lot's of shopping to do, that's going to be so fun.'

'Oh my own girl clothes? Mum might not let me be Saskia.'

'Oh no, gosh I'd forgot. You're only here for the weekend. Oh hell. What if your mum makes you be Ed? Oh shit, what have I done? It would be awful if you have to be Ed all the time. I've seriously messed up, messed you up.'

'I don't think I can go back. I hate being Ed, that's why I've been so sad because being a boy is so gross.'

'I can't imagine. Maybe mum can persuade your mum. Oh shitty knickers. I'm so sorry.'

'The Genie is out of the lamp. I'll not go back. It's not up to mum, it's up to me.'

'Can you be that strong?'

'Yes I think I can, I know I can. You and your mum have made me strong.'

'You go in my bathroom, I'll go in my parents en suite. I'll put clothes out for you, ballet stuff and I'll be back to help in case you don't get it, you know, which way they go on. I've got all this dance gear.'

I went into the bathroom and used the electric toothbrush, the brush-head with the purple band. I washed face and hands. When I came back into the bedroom I found laid out what I was to wear, white tights and a candy pink leotard and a pull on skirt in a lovely soft fabric to match the leotard. It was so pretty. I pulled on the tights, just as I had seen mum do and then the leotard, managing to find front and back using the label as my guide. I pulled on the little matching skirt. Jenn returned.

'Let's see you spin. Like this.' She demonstrated.

I tried to copy.

'You'll do. You'd hardly know you were a boy down there, your winkle must be quite small. You look terrific in that. Mum's going to do something about your hair, but after ballet. We are going to mum's hairdresser friend and she's going to make you more girly, more Saskia. Give you an urchin cut or something, or long bob.'

'What will mum say?' I was feeling a bit alarmed that mum wasn't being consulted at all.

'Oh mum will see to that, she's very persuasive. Besides they had a long chat yesterday. It's all OK for you to be a girl.'

I still wasn't sure, in fact I didn't want mum being persuaded, I wanted mum to agree, to welcome me as a daughter not to have a daughter foisted upon her. I seemed to be picked up in a Jennings whirlwind. I was spinning; such a lot of change all at once. I had arrived here yesterday as a boy almost in tears and already I was a ten year old girl.

I hardly knew what was going on. I liked it, in fact I loved what they were doing to me, but I was frightened that mum would want it all undone and she and dad if he ever came back, would hate me for becoming a girl even for just this weekend. I was just scared too, of meeting people, the ballet class and whoever else and yet my latent desires so long unfulfilled, drove me forward to be a girl.

Jenn changed right in front of me as though I was really a girl and put on her nearly identical ballet wear but in ice blue. 'Come on Saskia, come down and meet dad. Oh just a minute, your hair. I'll try something.'

She grabbed her brush in one hand and a spray can. 'Here we go.' She brushed until my hair was all smooth and brought over my face then she sprayed a big blob of cream onto her hand and worked that in to my hair pulling it up and letting it fall back and suddenly I had hair that looked far longer, and also was far higher on my head. 'Don't flatten it. It looks wild, like an urchin cut almost. I've done well. Come on Saskia.'

She took my hand and we went down together. This touching business was defo a girl thing and I would have to get used to it. Don't get me wrong, I really liked it. It was like coming home. I felt like I was a real person after all my years, well about six years, of feeling I wasn't a real person at all. All the same, going down and seeing her father was frightening. I mean women and girls are one thing, men are quite another.

We entered the kitchen together and her dad was already sitting drinking coffee and reading the paper. I felt my face growing red when he looked up.

'Hello Saskia. Come and sit down. Well we are all here now, so mum, shall we have our porridge?'

'You certainly will. Saskia, you do look nice, that pink really suits you. Just a plate of porridge, you have to go out with something in your tummies. Are you girls drinking tea or juice, squash?'

'I'll have tea please.' I say and Jenn gets up and goes for a glass of squash.

Breakfast is soon over. We go to the car and we are off to ballet. I'm suddenly really frightened. I sit in the back and Jenn is in the front, throwing advice back to me until Rebecca tells her to be quiet.

'Saskia is quite capable of doing everything she needs to do. Saskia, just try to do as the teacher asks. She won't expect you to immediately be a ballerina. It's like anything, you need teaching and practice and everyone starts from scratch. You'll be fine and you look gorgeous.'

We go in and Mrs Jennings talks to the teacher while Jenn teaches me how to put the ballet shoes on. I can hardly move my feet and they make you walk in a completely different way. Jenn taught me that as well and we go onto the dance floor.

'We have a new member. Saskia, step forward please.'

I stepped forward and the pupils said in Unison, 'Hello Saskia.'

I say hello and try to smile. I think I succeed.

'Right then girls. At the bar and Rosemarie, you lead you know the exercises. Right Saskia, that's a very good name for a dancer. So you're going to try out your new mum says.'

'She's not my mum! She's our neighbour and Jenny's my best friend.'

'Oh sorry, I misunderstood. As this is your first time, just follow what they do. They have been here quite a time, some, not all. If you can't do something give it a try but don't strain. I'll help you.'

For the next hour we did exercises and I liked it, I liked the clothes and the other girls too. There were two boys who did different things sometimes but I was surprised how much I could do. At the end I was pretty tired. The teacher had helped me quite a lot and while the others were finishing off, practising the basic positions, she guided me through them. I couldn't do the sixth at all but she was impressed she said with what I could do as a first timer. It would all come with practice and I was a promising student if a little late beginning she said.

'Will you come again Saskia?'

'Yes please.'

'Good girl.'

We changed into what Rebecca called street clothes. They gave me a mini skirt, red denim and a cream blouse. They were really lovely and I said so, but Jenn just said, 'What, those old things?'

We arrived at the hairdresser's just as Jenn had said. I noted the name of it, 'Beyond the Fringe' and I quite liked that. There were three girls inside and a young girl, with really dark brown hair came forward and greeted Mrs Jennings.

'This is our Saskia. She wants to grow her hair. I had thought an urchin cut but that would mean chopping her hair off. What do you suggest Diana?'

'I think we will just trim it up into a really girly style and show her how to do it.'

They took me to the basin and washed my hair and then she snipped away and just blew it dry. It was really nice when it was done and she showed me how to roll the brush and use the hair dryer at the same time. I sort of got it and Diana said it would come with practice. It seemed I had a lot to learn.

Chapter 5.

From there we went to the Mall.

We scampered out. 'Now you two, not too much excitement. I'm putting the car park ticket in the pocket of my handbag Saskia, so remember where won't you? Now up the escalator and the next one to the food hall. I think we'll have a bit of lunch first and a little talk about the future.'

We waited to be seated and eventually were taken to a table that was OK. Rebecca was quite fussy and told the girl she would not sit at two tables and I saw her sense, one was right by the food and the other close to the entrance. 'Too much toing and froing,' she said, 'we need a bit of privacy.'

We sat in like a booth in a corner. We went to make our choices from the buffet style self serve. I resisted taking too much as we could always go back and mum would never let us waste food.

We ate and then sat with our milk shakes.

'Let's get out of here girls, it's too hot. We'll go up on the roof garden.'

'I thought we were shopping mum?' Jenn said.

So we go up some stairs to the roof garden where you can see over the City. We found a seat in half shade.

'So a morning as Saskia. I'm worried about you. I mean it was fun dressing up last night and Jenn was a bit naughty doing that. You seem to like it. I want to understand. Is it nicer for you being Ed or Saskia, tell me honestly, and you keep your mouth shut Jenny.'

'It's being Saskia. It's what I've always wanted.'

'What you want to wear girl clothes or be Saskia?'

'I want to be Saskia and wear girl clothes. I feel right. I hate being Ed. It's been awful acting a part, pretending to be a boy because mum and dad, particularly dad, expected me to be one.'

'That's right mum she...'

'Hold your tongue Jenny. This is serious, not some game. So you feel better as Saskia? More like you should be?'

'Yes.'

'Positively? Definitely?'

'Oh so definitely. I've never been so happy.'

'I don't know how far to go with this. The thing is, you'll be staying with us for sometime. Your dad has apparently gone drilling oil in Mexico. We think he doesn't intend coming back. He left your mum a note and that's what it said.

'This name, Saskia. It's certainly a girl's name. Where did that come from?'

'Me,' Jenn says eager to take the credit.

'It's a no compromise name; I mean there's no mistaking it for being a boy's name. Very girly, classy. I like it but is it really what we are going to call you?'

'She loves the name mum.'

'Jenny, I shall not tell you again. I'm speaking to Saskia if that's to be her name. I have to understand what it is she wants, not you. Is it Saskia and being a girl?'

'That's what I would love, but will mum let me?'

Rebecca takes my hand and then takes my other hand, so we are face to face. 'You really and truly can't be Edward?'

'I hate being Edward.'

'That's what Lizzie told me. So Saskia then. Would you be Saskia at school?'

'Of course.'

Rebecca just looks at me as though trying to see into my head. There's silence apart from distant traffic and bird life among the rooftops. She sighs and I think she's going to say I can't be Saskia.

'Very well Saskia. Suddenly being a girl at school where all the children know you as Edward, will not be easy. There will be some children who want to bully and make fun, make trouble. Then there's the toilets, boys or girls.'

'The girls', I always sit anyway and if I'm a girl why would I, how could I go in the boys'?'

'Yes, well I hope that won't present any difficulty. There are games too. I will have to discuss that with school. What are we going to tell people?'

'I...haven't thought.'

'I don't like lying. I think if I have read the Internet sites properly, you have a girl brain and a boy body. So why don't we say, you have girl parts and boy parts and you like being a girl best. What do you think Saskia?'

'That sounds the best solution. It's difficult because everyone will be curious.'

'Are you strong enough? It will take courage.'

'I am strong enough. I will be. I don't care what people think. Anyway, I'm not doing any harm.'

'No but some may think you are. You're to tell me if you get upset.'

'What about mum? What does she say? Does she mind?'

'Your mum told me yesterday that if being a girl made you happy then she was happy for you to be a girl. She said you had been unhappy for far too long.'

'Where is my mummy?'

'Saskia. There's more bad news. You have to be brave now.' She takes my hand across the table. Filtered light from the shading tree falls across our arms making a continually shifting pattern as the leaves flutter and branches move in the breeze. Time seems to stand still and I'm waiting for whatever this grave news will be.

'First of all I would like to know, do you like staying with us? Do you like having Jenn as a sister.'

'I love her. She's my bestie, always has been. And you always welcomed me and you've been kind. It's like my second home.'

'Well we are fond of you too. I could never have another baby, so having you in the house has been good for me and for Jenny. So we are all happy there then. What if you were to live with us permanently? How would that be?'

'What never go home? What about mum, will she live with us too?'

'I have to tell you some awful news now Saskia. I went and saw your mum last night, while you two were playing up stairs. She wasn't at all well. I think you know she was very sad, that's why she sent you round to us. She asked me whether you could live with us and of course I said you were welcome for as long as whatever. She handed me a letter and in it she has asked me to look after you. We have had that agreement for a long time, that if either of us died, then your mum would have looked after Jenn and I would look after you. It's in our wills.

'I came home, and then for some reason, because I was worried, I went back. I found your mum unconscious. I called the ambulance and they arrived pretty quickly. Even so, come and sit by me Saskia.' I moved onto the bench beside her. 'Saskia there's no good way I can say this.' I could hear by her voice that it was terrible news. 'Your mum died on the way to hospital. I'm really sorry. She was my best friend. What she told me was, she wants you to be happy living with us and if that is being Saskia which brings happiness, then you are Saskia.'

I looked at her and my face broke in bits, my throat hurt and my eyes even ached and my cheeks crinkled up and then I let out this terrible moan and sobbed. Jenn sat the other side and threw her arms around me too. Rebecca almost crushed me, perhaps trying to squash the torment out of me. I knew other people were looking. I didn't care. It must have been at least five minutes before I could speak.

'It's my fault, because I'm so girly, because I want to be a girl. I killed my mum!' I howl again.

'Shhh Saskia, there, there. No that wasn't the reason. Your mum, first Nick dying, then your dad being heartbroken and the rows and then leaving, it was too much for her. Her last thoughts were of you. She wanted you to be happy. She said, and we had discussed you often enough thinking that one day, you would want to be a girl, she said to me, take care of my darling Edward whatever happens. I promised saying silly things like of course nothings going to happen. All the time, she knew she was going to die. So you see, she loved you deeply, but sometimes people just can't go on. Life seems just too difficult.'

I dissolved. I just sat and sobbed and I saw through my tear filled eyes other people watching and then moving away. Soon there was only a couple left on the roof besides us. I don't know how long I sobbed but Rebecca and Jenn clung to me all that time. At last I was being hugged and loved but I would rather have had my mum back.

After a time I managed to recover my breathing enough to say, 'I knew she was very sad. That's why she was so cross. And then I went into her room and we cuddled sitting on the bed and she kissed me and held me and all the time, she must have been thinking about dying and leaving me. She told me to come to you.'

'And then she phoned, asking if I would keep you. I said of course I would, she knew that, hadn't we agreed on that often? Yes we had she said, just checking. I knew something was seriously wrong. That's why I went down there. I called the ambulance. Then I came back to make sure you were all right and ordered you not to leave the house. I'm sorry I couldn't save her.'

I sat stunned. I couldn't speak. I didn't have anything in my head to say or ask.

'Jenny, go down and get a tray of drinks, whatever you want, whatever you think Saskia will have. An Americano for me, grande. You have money, I'll pay you back later.'

Jenny went quickly. 'So Saskia. You want to stay with us and be Jenn's sister?'

143

I manage to nod. She kisses me on my forehead and then my cheek and holds me very tightly.

'And it's still this girl thing. You're sure?'

'Mum really wanted me to be Saskia?'

'Oh yes, she wanted whatever you wanted, whatever would make you happy. I said so already. She was just waiting for you to come out with it. But it had to come from you. Well Jenn took care of that. But if that will make you happy, then we will do our best to make it happen. So this afternoon, first we must do a little retail therapy, just enough for now and when you feel better, when you are over the shock, we'll do more. And we will have to do your bedroom out at ours, make it suitable for a girl. You can help paint or stencil and make curtains. Then we will have to think about school. You are both in your last year at juniors. Perhaps it would be best for you both to move to a new school, as you are a new person. You're a bit frightened of my husband, your new father. You can call him dad or daddy or use his name Simon. Don't be frightened. He is just as happy for you to be our daughter as I am. Saskia, you must tell me everything. What you like, what you don't like. What frightens you and pleases you. If you are ever unhappy about something, don't keep it a secret. Don't ever think you are like just staying with us as a guest. You will be our daughter, equal to Jenny and what you like is just as important as what she likes. You are not a poor relation like, well, have you seen the film 'Jane Eyre'?'

'Yes. Her cousins were horrible.'

'It is not going to be like that. All I ask is that you try to be good and you are. You do your best at school, the same as I want from Jenn. So I wonder where she's got to? Oh here she is.'

'Mum this lot took all my money. So cough up mum. I bought meringues to give as a sugar fix.'

She sat next to me and kissed my cheek.

'Thank you, thanks both of you. Rebecca, I need T blockers. I can't be a man.' I say.

'Well you have me there. I will have to look that up. Is it a drug?'

'Testosterone blockers. It can be a regular injection or an implant. If I don't get it, I go through male puberty and some things can't be undone.'

'Well we can't have that. Shopping first, then we'll go home and you can tell me all you know. You've researched this haven't you?'

'Inside and out. T blockers are really important though.'

'Then you shall have them. First, well after we have eaten this sugar and cream naughtiness my daughter has bought with my money, knickers and a few clothes. On another day, you two girls can shop together, choose all your own stuff as long as you are sensible.'

'What will happen to our house?'

'It will be sold I imagine and at least half will come to you. It will have to be invested, kept in trust for your future. We will have to bring all your personal things to ours, your laptop and anything else, your teddy, perhaps your desk and maybe your wardrobe. We need to buy you some girl furniture too, a vanity for one thing.'

'What if dad comes back?'

'We cross that bridge when we come to it but if we adopt you, it's for good. He can't just come in and out of your life on a whim. There are two alternatives, one is adoption and permanent, the other is as our foster child. Either way the authorities are going to investigate us to see we are fit parents for you. Even if we just foster I think it would be difficult for dad to reclaim you. What are your thoughts?'

'Adoption. I'd like to be part of your family forever. My dad doesn't like me.'

We shopped. I just let them do what they thought best; the only decisions I made were on colours. I totally refused anything green and black was too depressing. Somehow we went home laden. We spent an hour in the evening just peeling and cutting off labels. Then they were all put away in the chest in what was to be my room. Jenn had enough school wear for me to share. It was our last term at junior school, so buying new stuff would have been a waste, especially as there was only a month till term end. I didn't mind, I liked wearing Jenn's stuff. I was living, reacting, but only just, catatonic almost.

Jenn and I went to bed early. I cried myself to sleep, Jenn cuddled into my back and her hand on my tummy.

Chapter 6.   Saskia's Tale

As happy as I was suddenly becoming Saskia, the death of my mum and the virtual eradication of my family in a matter of months, sent me into a downward spiral. I went to my old home and collected a few items I wanted to keep. I had to be a realist. I kept photos, anything really personal, mum's jewellery, her perfume and a scarf I had secretly treasured. There was some good cutlery and china that we packed in an old trunk to be stored in the Jennings loft, my new home. The rest, after having been referred by Rebecca to dad, was going for auction. Then the house would be sold and all trace of the Simpson family would have gone. The next week I was kept off school. I was silent except for answers to questions and then I responded with the minimum possible.

That week I stayed home from school, I came to breakfast in PJs or a nightie and then Rebecca would take me up and dress me, educating me in how to wear things and what to wear. Everywhere she went I went. I helped in the kitchen. We made curtains for my bedroom. I was almost silent but I would do what I was asked. We kept busy all week.

When Jenn came home I would be with her. Of course we slept together. That was such a comfort, having another human warm and soft and affectionate. I think it was

Jenn that brought me round, but it was not just months; it was years before I really felt better and had whole days when I didn't cry.

I went to school as Saskia and of course it caused a stir. Some were really nice about it and some were frankly horrid. Luckily Jenn had a good group, well I was already part of it and after the first shock and the fascination of some who wanted to know everything, I was accepted as Saskia. Mostly the teachers were quite good too. Some of the kids were always horrid and while we waited for Rebecca to collect us, one or two of the mothers made nasty remarks. I was learning very quickly that being human and different was not an easy path.

If they thought that would make me go back to being Edward, they were very much mistaken, but I suspect they didn't care. All they wanted to do was bully because I did not conform.

I loved my school uniform. It was not the prettiest, grey pleated skirt and navy blazer and a white blouse, but to me, after the boy uniform, it was delicious. White ankle socks and black Mary Janes completed the outfit.

It was not surprising that some found it difficult. It's not everyday that a child defies nature and conventions and becomes the opposite of what they have been or are considered to be.

Almost the first thing Rebecca did for me in that first dreadful week was take me to the GP and explain things. Urgent of course were T blockers, which I had to explain to them both. Testosterone is what makes a boy child into a man, alters boys so they becoming bigger in everyway, muscles, bones, hair on the body and face, chest and even back. Yuck. That's an awful thought. One of the worst things in male puberty is of course, breaking voice that can occur sort of any time between twelve and sixteen. That is the hardest thing to correct, as I pointed out to Dr Sims and what gives transsexuals away more than anything else. It can be corrected surgically but with mixed results, or it can be voice therapy so people learn to communicate in a higher range. It's cheaper to stop all this happening with T blockers.

T blockers I told him, are reversible. Stop them prior to having surgery to the downstairs area and male hormones kick in and male development will kick in. T blockers therefore just delay the fatal male puberty and give a breathing space so a child can take time to decide, male or female. I knew I would not change my mind, but one has to follow the rules. T blockers are therefore essential.

Dr Sims did some reading and phoning and I received the Ts. That was the biggest worry wiped away. I would have to wait till I was at least sixteen to get oestrogen that would make me more girly, breast development being the big thing.

By the time the summer holidays came, I was safe from maleness, living as Saskia with my own clothes although, like most sisters, we wore each other's stuff. We did most things together but Jenn was sportier than me. She played tennis and she put up with me being useless. However, she did say I was improving and I was. It got so we could play doubles with her mum and dad. I expressed an interest in cycling and they bought me a racing bike, I don't like to think how expensive that was, but it must have been a few hundred. When I went on a downer, Jenn was there, distracting me, making me take an interest in a game of Scrabble or a race to the shops on our bikes for sweets. I may owe my life to her, my dear sister.

My room was done out, similar to Jenn's, but we often slept together. Rebecca didn't mind. She said we were joined at the hip, like Siamese twins. I was frightened at first that seeing her all the time, we might get on each other's nerves, but we didn't and still don't. We just enjoy being together all the time. Yet we give each other space now and again but every day with Jenn is just another great day.

Sometimes though, I haven't been good company. I have found mum's death much more difficult than Nick's. I suppose that is just as it would be. And the shock of becoming an orphan, even though I was living with a family even more dear to me than my own, raised some difficulties. I mean it was me who was the difficult one. Sometimes I was very quiet and they would try to bring me out and then I would get sulky. I couldn't help it. Much as I was euphoric at being Saskia, the shock of losing Nick and then my mum, easily outweighed the joy of being myself.

My schoolwork dipped, not surprising Simon said as he looked at my end of year report. 'Even so Saskia, very well done. We expect great things when you move to your new school.'

The one thing that people would have found surprising was my transition to adopting the identity of a girl, Jenn's sister, caused me no problems at all. I had I supposed studied Jenn and she became the model for the new me. I had always been an 'honorary' girl in their household so the difference was just in my clothing. The one thing I found confusing at first, just for a few days was buttons, hands doing the opposite of what a boys do. Otherwise there was little change, well managing a skirt being the most important, sitting more carefully. I had always kept my knees together anyway and the rest just seemed obvious.

School finished and we two girls then had to attend for interview and entrance exam to a private school, girls only. We were accepted. Brilliant and what's more their uniform is not bad, pleated winter skirts and a plain French blue blazer. We got fitted out with new, but Rebecca warned us, in future we would be going to the schools second hand fair held twice a year. Who cares if the uniform is second hand or my hockey stick isn't new?

Four weeks into the summer break and next week we are departing for the holiday in Brittany France, that's my new family, the Jennings. It was debateable whether I become a Jennings or remain a Simpson. Anyway for this holiday I'm a Simpson, but I am being officially adopted. That's the option I chose. I don't want dad coming back with a new wife, liking the new Saskia and laying claim. I'm sorry but dad and me are over.

The dreadful events have passed. I tell Rebecca, I'm over the worst and I'm happy as Saskia, as I should be, an all-new wardrobe and a newly decorated bedroom, parents that indulge me, encourage me and hug. Family life is so different. Above all I'm happy being a Jennings, I just wish mum hadn't swallowed those pills. I try not to think about it as it brings on tears. Jenn is like a sniffer dog, she detects a downer immediately and does her best to distract me, suggests doing something or asks her mum, my new mum to take us somewhere, or we get the bikes out and pedal it off.

When we all got stuck in we finished my room in a week. Jenn and I still sleep together though because I'm still really unhappy in the quiet times and, I miss my mum.

I can't get rid of the thought, though people say I'm wrong, I should have stayed with mum and she would not have done what she did. I feel so guilty. I also feel she was selfish. Her love of me should have been enough that she would want to carry on living, just to look after me. Suicide is a terrible thing, not for the victim but for those left behind. At first I thought, well, she couldn't be bothered, didn't love me enough to stay alive. Then I thought, she made plans for me, knew that Rebecca would take me and love me. I wish she hadn't had to overdose though. We would have made it through. Rebecca says that sometimes people come to a brick wall and they either batter themselves senseless against it or end their lives. She told me that it was not my fault and I am not to think it was. Easier said than done. Sometimes it's as if a dark cloud comes down and I just burst into tears.

There were lots of people at her funeral and I was the chief mourner. I read a lesson and a eulogy. Rebecca also did a tribute. Dad didn't come. He sent flowers. He also wrote me a long letter about not being able to cope with Nick's death and them being so close. He'd written to Rebecca and given permission for them to adopt me. He was aware of my change of sex too and he wished Saskia well and asked for photos. First I thought, get lost, I was so bitter, he had deserted us and I still think, caused mum's death more than me. After a few days more, I thought about it and studied myself in the mirror. I dressed in what Jenn and I thought was my best outfit. Simon took about fifteen photos and as a family, we picked what were voted as the best five to email.

I have to say, he didn't email back for about four days and I was so angry with him. Finally a reply came and he did say I looked gorgeous and when, if, he came back to England, he would be proud to take me out. Dad made no protest at my name change, threw it back at me, 'whatever makes you happy.'

That sort of put a line under my old life, ruled across, dealt with and on with a new chapter as a Jennings. You would think he would have hated that I wasn't carrying his name.

Life is terrific; I mean good, excellent apart from the scars that the death of Nick followed by suicide of my mum leave. I burst into tears at the drop of a hat. I hope I shall grow out of that.

OK me being Saskia is a bit of a pretence because unfortunately I have boy bits, but in every other way I am Saskia. We managed to get a new passport by queuing at the

Passport office, which has a nice photo of Saskia Jennings, not Edward and it says female.

We went privately to a clinic that deals with us 'misfits'. The NHS one in London is so booked up and the waiting time is something over a year. Anyway, the important thing is I shall not become a man. The psychiatrist made me do lots of tests to find out my mental state and sexual orientation. Apparently I did OK on that.

You should have seen my complete new wardrobe. No boy clothes at all. We had a ceremonial burning and that was so good and Jenn and I danced around the blaze as her dad stoked the flames. Many other personal effects went on the fire as well, family stuff. You can't keep everything. It's ones memory that counts.

I considered the day I moved in with the Jennings my rebirth and I try as much as possible to shut out all previous memories. Of course I fail, the brain works in a mysterious way and sometimes one comes to a stop, something, you're not even sure what, triggers a memory that carries one back in time. There's no gainsaying memory and I have plenty of them.

I used my bike to get over that, exerting every once of strength, cycling sometimes thirty miles. That's something I do better than Jenn, biking. She can't stay with me.

From the very first I loved being Saskia. I woke in the morning and even if the sun wasn't out, it was in my heart. Before, when I was Ed, my world seemed pretty monotone. Like one of those days when there's uniform grey cloud and no blue, and nothing in a landscape shines out. Those day when one feels that it is you against the World and wonder why we struggle so to remain here.

Now I think, my life is like a Disney cartoon the bluebirds sing, the flowers sway and pop, and even small creatures say, hello Saskia. Yes I know that's daft but it's how I feel. Life has taken on a new meaning. I'm so much happier as a person and I like other people more and I'm gaining in confidence every day.

Before I was frightened to say I liked this or that, like girly films like the Princess Diaries or the Parent Trap because boys weren't supposed to like those things, but I identified with the heroines and loved them. I liked pretty, clothes, furnishings, and views. I liked girl sports and adored rhythmic gymnastics with the costumes and the ribbons and hoops as well as the synchronised swimming, but I couldn't say. Now I can just be myself. People think it's just about the clothes or attracting boys. It's not. Oh yes the clothes, look I want to be female, my brain is female and the brain dictates my likes and dislikes. Girls, most girls like pretty clothes and want to be like other girls and express their femininity. So do I.

Boys, I don't know. In my mind, like lots of girls, I like boys, like them, admire a handsome boy. That's not like I want to have sex with them. Will I ever? I can't say, I don't know, so that's not a reason why I wanted to be a girl. I just identify with girls and all girl things.

I've taught my new family all about trans, well Simon doesn't take that much interest. Men are so different, shy of sex or sexual organs, really. It's as though a ton of shingle has been poured on that section of their brain that deals with emotions or love. Oh they know passion and lust, bravado and machismo. That's why I think, and I think about difference a lot in trying to understand myself, men rush us into war, grown up, educated men, to prove themselves even if it's just sending other men to their deaths.

So you want examples I suppose to support my grand assertions. OK, Blair and Bush rushing us into war in Iraq. The two of them in their bomber jackets like regular pilots. How stupid they were when I watched this film Simon was looking at about that Iraq thing. Cameron involving us in Libya and after that disaster wanting involvement in Syria. Like that other film I looked for an essay on Democracy and Dictatorship, Hitler, Mussolini and the Japanese in WW2. Leaders stalking about all stiff and brave, but they weren't the ones on the front line. I excuse our leaders in that one because we were defending the weak from monstrous regimes. Putin in Russia, cultivating his man of action image although he's really a tiny little shrimp but then the EU severely provoked him with its overtures to Ukraine. I could go much deeper but it would bore you. It is in the male human's nature to fight even if it's by proxy, sending young men to their deaths. I think it would be a better World if leaders like Blair had to get in the boxing ring with someone like Saddam Hussein and fight until a knockout. The truth is Iraq was a better place to live under that tyrant than it has been for the last thirteen dreadful years. The same applies to Libya and Syria. Simon says I spend too much time on my computer, but that's how I learn all this stuff.

So Simon is content to learn third hand about trans but Rebecca and Jenn have been right into it reading the science sites. Rebecca has promised she will make sure I have the best treatment. I'm so happeeee! Knowing I will not grow up a man is such a relief for me because I have this female brain.

So we go to France, all in Simon's BMW and it's a whole new adventure. My passport is offered at immigration and I wonder whether some one will pop out and say, 'Oi you're not really a girl!' but they don't of course.

It's super having a sister. We explore the boat together after we've eaten dinner and we watch England and the Isle of Wight slip away beside the ship and the sun disappear and we go to our cabin to sleep. The bunks are quite narrow and there's a continuous hum from the engines. We think we'll never sleep. We go in the small shower room together and figure out how to work the funny shower thing without boiling ourselves. I've gotten used to Jenn seeing my boy thing. It's quite small and doesn't get any bigger. Thank goodness.

Jenn never mentions it. Dear Jenn I couldn't wish for a better sister. We sleep soundly until Rebecca rouses us for breakfast in the morning. We eat full English because Simon says; we shall not have lunch as such, just a snack.

Chapter 7.   Saskia's Tale

That holiday in Brittany brought me round. It seemed as though leaving England I had also left my troubles behind. We stayed at a gîte somewhere near Landivisiau. It was a really rural area with not a lot of entertainments like theme parks or anything, but we went to lots of different beaches and we did walks and went to places like Brest. One day we went on a really long trip to Bayeux to see the famous tapestry. To tell the truth, although it was really interesting as an account of the events leading up to the invasion of England in 1066 by William the Conqueror, made at the time, I thought it would be bigger. I expected it to be at least six feet high but I guess it was only about thirty inches. Anyway it was very interesting. Surprisingly on a Saturday morning, the museum was quite empty. We expected a queue and there was none.

There was a market. We bought some peculiar looking bread, by the slice cut from an enormous loaf and some fruit gateaux, the French make them so well. We looked for cheese, for which France is supposed to be famed but we couldn't find a fromagerie (cheese shop). Peculiar.

Lots of places sold moules frites, (mussels and chips) and I think my new dad and I almost lived on them. Mussels are fiddly little things to eat but tasty. Rebecca, I haven't got round to calling her mum and my sister Jenn usually had something more exotic. Everywhere they sold crepes like pancakes but you can have savoury as well as fruit. They were OK but not that exciting. I class them with that abomination, a wrap, that piece of slightly soggy cardboard popular these days, like the taco, poor man's food. The sweet crepes were best.

The holiday was really a bonding session. They were getting to know me and I was getting to know them. Every family is different, just little things people do that make a difference taken altogether, the food they eat, whether they drink at meal times, loo seat up or down, clean plates or allowed to leave something, attitudes to animals or conservation. Those sorts of things. If you don't cotton on to how others do things, it can be a nuisance, an annoyance to them, so I made a note, to only be told once and to change to fit in.

My new dad was great fun. He is a great tease of us girls, telling us all sorts that aren't true, as a joke, waiting for our horrified reaction. He treated me the same as Jenn and we played lots of games on the beach, cricket and boules or petanque, I think they are the same and we even built sandcastles. We walked around a lake in the countryside and played hide and seek and we had picnics.

It was a really happy two weeks, but in the back of my head I still carried the memory of my last afternoon with mum.

I wish I had known how depressed she had been and perhaps I could have saved her. As much as I love my new life, I would have given it all up to have mum back. I lay sunbathing, covered in the sunblock Rebecca made us smother ourselves with and silently cried for my mum. I wouldn't let them know how sad I felt, because that would have brought them down. They would have felt too, that I wasn't happy and actually I was happier than I can remember ever being in my life, lying there in my little bikini with the empty bra. I just wanted my mum.

Two weeks seemed to rush by. We were back on the ferry in no time at all and heading north on our way home. In ten days we would be in our new school.

We saw the headmistress about my status and the fact that for obvious reasons I needed special treatment or to see whether there were ways round it.

I said that I thought it was best to be totally upfront about my status to the other girls. That way I hoped there would be no nasty whispers, no anxious parents wanting me ostracised, no Christians campaigning against trans and saying it was against the will of God or any such rubbish. I knew the truth would get out anyway, it always does so better to be honest from the start and explain and allay any silly fears. Mind you, it doesn't hurt to colour the truth

I read a lot about attacks on trans in the USA and I wonder why they get in so much trouble. I know America is not UK and the Land of the Free isn't free. Religion is much stronger and faiths preach against people like me. So I'm keeping my fingers crossed that I'll have no trouble. Americans hate the Taliban and IS, Muslim zealots and yet some of their preachers are awful, preaching hate against people like me or against abortion and even killing abortion doctors and trans and gay people. I don't understand how otherwise intelligent people, who's God taught love of others, can be so horrid.

Rebecca bless her, has found these briefs on the Internet that will contain my genitalia to be worn when I wear anything revealing. They are not that comfortable. Usually my cotton panties are enough restriction. I wish it wasn't there. I hate it; I even imagine cutting it off myself. Of course I won't, I don't want to die but if they would take me into hospital tomorrow and do it, I would leap for joy.

We start back to school the first full week of September. Everything is fine. I'm not challenged at all, I'm just another girl and then of course someone from my old school recognises me and the whispering begins. It is not long before I am challenged at lunchtime. This girl Summer Early who I quite like speaks openly in front of everyone.

'Are you really a boy Saskia?'

'Don't hold back,' says Jenn, defensive of me. 'How can you ask a question like that?'

'Just people are whispering.'

'Well I was a sort of boy,' I say, my face burning. 'I have boy bits and girl bit's and if you ask which bits, I'll not answer and I might give you a slap. As my brain is like a girl's brain I choose to be a girl. Why do you ask? Are you really a boy?'

'Course not.' She says turning red.

'Only I heard you are. I don't think you are. I think you just need to learn to be tactful.'

There were a few sniggers. Then this girl Caroline Mason said, 'Yes Summer, you're really rude.'

After that I seemed to have no more trouble. Teachers were very watchful for any bullying and we had regular talks on citizenship that contained warnings about bullying and zero tolerance. We were all told to report bullying of anyone.

I still wasn't good at sports but with encouragement I got into hockey, playing left full back. Of course my sister is really good and plays left wing. She is very quick and she inspires me to try harder. We practice together and in the end

I'm not bad. I like hockey and the little skirts we wear I love, like our tutus but best of all is the team spirit.

October and I take to my own bed. At last I feel strong enough to sleep alone. I miss being in with Jenn but I feel I have to learn to have time on my own. We do homework separately but we test each other and we compare notes taken in class. So I guess we have an advantage over other people. Anyway, we don't care and we come out top of the class. That's how it is as we move from year to year.

The next thing that happened after starting at St Hilda's was the selling of the Simpson house and a battle over mum's will. She had left everything to Nick and me thinking that we would of course survive her. As it was of course the house was in mum's and dad's name. Dad's solicitor maintained that it therefore all went to him. Our solicitor argued that half should come to me and eventually dad gave in. I was therefore an heiress.

There was also a matter of mum's life insurance. The Company argued that they didn't pay out on suicides if they occurred within two years of the commencement of the policy. Our solicitor wrote and told them that policy was five years old, and the amendment that was made eighteen months ago, was imposed by the company, so sucks. After a lot of letters that cost me three thousand, they paid up. My education was therefore assured. I wouldn't have a student loan and I told my parents that I would also pay for Jenn. It was the least I could do not that they wanted any payment.

After three years I was just about normal. The sudden tears had stopped although there was still a hole in my heart where mum and even my brother had been. That emptiness will always be there I fear but as they say, time is a healer and as time goes by, the pain will become less intense and the guilt I feel over mum's suicide will lessen. My adoptive family have been brilliant.

Chapter 8.   Saskia's Tale

My fourteenth birthday arrived. This year for the first time I was having a proper birthday party. Dad, that's what I now called Simon, has suggested that I get over my fear of heights by going to one of the tree walks, this one Go Ape in Thetford Forest, there were eight of us girls in two cars, all giggling nervously and having lots of trips to the loo before getting fitted with safety harnesses.

We had a lesson on how to use them, making sure one of our two hook things was always hooked on. Follow that and one is quite safe, though it's still pretty scary, standing on a tiny platform fifty feet up and looking at the next hazard.

It brought back memories of the climbing wall, the last party Nick had before his death where I had conquered fear and found the courage to climb to the top. It was that event that I think brought Nick and I to an understanding of each other. I wished he could have been with us. He would have loved it.

Anyway we all did it and none of us chickened. There was a minor hiatus at the place where we had to swing through space into a cargo net and Rani a beautiful Indian girl would not make up her mind to go. In the end, it was Jenn who stood on the platform and made sure she was hooked on, then one, two, three, go and shoved her off shrieking into the void. She bounced into the net clutched to it and burst into giggles before unhitching and moving forward. Jenn was really good at leading and was captain of the under fifteens hockey and cricket teams as well as being my rival in class.

After that fun we went to a burger bar where you could order different burgers, have toasted buns and other options and, best of all, proper chips. It was really good and a brill party. Thanks to Dad and Mum who drove us in two cars. Eight girls and they put up with it, though dad said it was six girls too many. I feel sure he didn't mean it.

Three weeks after that, I received a letter from America. My heart skipped more than a beat and I thought I was going to be sick. Becca as I now call my new mum, I still can't bring myself to say mum, though sometimes I do by sort of mistake and blush after, said as I stared at it, "Would you like me to open that for you?'

'No thanks. I will. I'm just taking my time. Well Becca, here goes. A letter can't hurt can it?'

Jenn moved closer. How I love my sister. I'm so lucky to have her. I sometimes think if there'd been no Jenn, I'd have had nowhere to go.

I slit open the airmail with the US mail logo and stamps with a cat on one and a dog on another, the US pets series. Well at least the stamps are nice.

I open with trepidation. I fear that it may tell of my real dad's death or he may use my wrong name or some other bad news. It may not even be from dad. I've not heard from him for two years.

A photo falls out, dad with a woman with red, obviously dyed hair and a small child in his arms. So it looks as though he has started a new family. I don't even care. I read the letter.

Dear Sasha, (he can't even get my name right)

I realise that you probably never expected nor wanted to hear from your dad after how things were when I left. Then there were the quarrels over the house and your mum's insurances and you sure got me there.

Anyway, no grudges. I'm settled in Texas, as you see from the address on the back, Corpus Christi. We have a bungalow on stilts, so we park the cars under it. It's on stilts in case we get a bad hurricane hit and it floods. We are about sea level.

Anyway I made rig captain at last and we are working for Pemex, the Mexican state company and I've sent a photo of me and Madison my new wife and Michael, our two year old son.

Madison said I should write and connect, that I should not let the old wounds fester. I was like a bear with a sore head after Nick died and said things I shouldn't and yes I regret. Your mum is on my conscience. It was a terrible thing she did and I feel I'm pretty well responsible for that. I also said and did some pretty rotten things to you when you needed me most. Trouble is we can't go back and undo. I left you and you are almost an orphan, but luckily our good neighbours have looked after you. I hope you're doing fine as we are.

I'd like for you to drop me a line from time to time with a photo or two and news of how you're going. I hope well. You were always a *clever kid and I should have loved you for that alone even if I didn't understand.*

Just realised, I spelled your name wrong. See your old dad is still rubbish when it comes to using a pen.

I hope you'll drop me a line sometime with photos.

Love Dad. Xx

I leant back in my kitchen chair and found Becca watching me. I passed the letter to her and she leant back against the kitchen worktop and read. I waited for her verdict before saying anything. A sunbeam lit up the back of her head and her hair took on the appearance of a halo. Well she had been a saint in my life.

My first reaction to the letter was annoyance because apparently it was Madison who told him to write and he got my name wrong, and then couldn't be bothered to start over.

Becca read and said, 'Can Jenn read this?'

'Of course.' Becca passed the letter to Jenn. I waited for her verdict.

She finished reading. 'Well he's not asking for anything. Just wants to hear from you. I think that shows you must be on his mind.'

'What do you think about Madison telling him to write?'

'Ah that's upsetting you. I thought it might. Well look, you know men, they are not very good at emotional stuff. I suspect he said something about you, perhaps wondering how you were. She would have told him to write. They are probably both curious to know how you are, what you look like. There's nothing wrong with that is there?'

'No I spose not. As long as it's at a distance. I don't want him coming over and trying to lay claim. Mum would still be here if he hadn't gone like that.'

'Yes probably. Nothing can make up for losing your mum.'

'Becca, no of course Becca, but I want to say I love you just as much, perhaps more than mum, it's just different with you and of course I'm older and see things differently. I never call you mum, but that is how I think of you, the best mum I could have. I love my new family and I'm so happy to be with you, dad, mum and my darling sister Jenn.'

'That's nice to hear. You know we all love you don't we Jenn.'

'The best sister I could have, I should say so. If we'd come out of the womb together, it couldn't be any better.'

'I want to call you mum. May I?'

'Of course. That would mean so much to me.'

She came to the table as I stood and we embraced.

'Thank you Saskia, now as your mum, I hope you're going to reply and send photos, some of those from a month ago when we went to the theatre, the ones I took and perhaps if you get your makeup on, we'll take a couple and see if we have a lovely portrait. What about one of you in the hockey team? That would be good as he was so keen on sport.'

'Mm OK. Yes I'd like him to know that I'm thriving.'

'Yeah and beautiful.' Jenn said.

'Come on, it's a nice day. Let's do the photos and show him what he's missing. I don't think much of Madison's hair do you?' Jenn says laughing.

'Miaow.' I say.

Chapter 9.   Saskia's Tale

I glammed up and posed for Becca my photographer and Jenn her studio assistant.

That's the benefit of digital, take as many as you like and discard the nasties and idiot shots. In the end we had three quite artistic looking shots, one with me leaping in the air, my hair all in flight and quite a nice smile on my face. I selected three other photos to send, one of me playing hockey, one from our summer holiday in a bikini, sitting on the sand and exhibiting my long slim legs and another of Jenn and me, our heads close together back to back. Lastly, us as a family. That should show him what he's missing I thought. Yes I still felt bitter towards him. He can see I have risen from the ashes of that for me, loveless home.

I wrote a short note just saying I was surprised to hear from him and glad to see things were going well in the states. I congratulated him on becoming rig captain, so whatever my real thoughts, I sounded nice.

In truth, I was nice. I had almost forgiven him for everything. Even over mum's death, one can't be held responsible for the suicide of another. Ultimately in that situation, the future of someone is in their own hands, whatever the circumstances. I know with mum, it wasn't just his leaving; it was probably me and certainly the death of

Nick. All the same, he ought to have been more supportive of mum and me.

This year, my sixteenth on this earth and it's crucial for we have our General Certificate of Education exams, eleven subjects in all and Jenn and I are aiming at getting all A stars. We don't have to, I mean we can go in the sixth form and study for our A levels, with less good results and it is our success in A levels that really dictates how good a University we get to. It's more a matter of pride and a bit of competition between the two of us.

We study hard, helping each other, soaking up the knowledge. We also play sport and we belong to drama club and chess club and the debating society. So life is pretty full on and mum and dad spend time running around for us and waiting about.

We debate with a boy's school, St Joseph's and there's a guy named Ralph who's interested in me, but although he's nice, I'm not ready for that. Jenn has a boy, Ben and they've been out a few times. I'm a bit jealous but then she tells me she is dumping him. She can't be bothered to go out with someone just for the sake of saying she has a boy friend. There's nothing wrong with him, she says but what's the point, she's happier with me.

That's so good to hear and it's the way I feel about her. We have a lot of living to do and a lot of people to meet in the future. We just bounce off each other and actually, neither of us are ready for sex or even heavy petting, kissing and fumbling around. For me it's a no-no until I have my bottom surgery. From somewhere mum has got oestrogen patches. I apply them Saturday and Wednesday and guess what? I have breasts. After four months I have breasts, only small perhaps an A but breasts. I show Jenn and Becca, mum as I call her at last. They are impressed and pleased and we do a lot of hugging, Jenn is now a size B so I'm not that very far behind her. It's absolutely wonderful and painful. I love my body, well most of it.

I have to go to the NHS clinic in London once a year. They haven't time to see patients more often. It's very underfunded with long waiting times. What should be eighteen weeks from referral by General Practitioner to consultation in the clinic, is sometimes fifteen months and more, A long time for desperate children and those experiencing puberty or trying to avoid it. I'm lucky, I have good intelligent parents who look after me and know how to circumnavigate officialdom.

I bind my breasts as they would frown on drugs obtained probably illegally. I wait in a room that is uninspiring after reporting to reception. I'm dressed in a denim mini and pumps and a cream blouse, sleeveless with some detailing on the shoulders. I'm called in.

The consultant looks me up and down. She asks, 'Saskia Simpson?'

'Saskia Jennings. I've taken my adoptive parents name. I think mum wrote to you.'

'Very well. I'll have your file altered.' She strikes out Simpson and writes Jennings.

'So tell me how things are going.'

'I'm happy.'

'Just that?'

'What more is there to say? I'm top of my class in my all girls' school, studying for my GCSEs and I hope to get A stars. I love my sister Jenn and I love my parents. I play hockey and I bicycle.'

'No regrets about taking this journey to be outwardly female, knowing that internally you will remain male?'

'I regret only that I shall never be able to have children. I'd love to have a baby one day. I know that's not going to happen.'

'Have you a boyfriend?'

'No. I know a few boys but although we sometimes go out in a mixed gang, it's mainly girls we mix with.'

'How do you feel about boys?'

'Most of the ones I know are OK, but they're my age, a bit immature, going through puberty. They're a bit silly. One or two are really nice.'

'Do you pet, kiss?'

'No.'

'Why?'

'Because I'm not in that sort of relationship with any of them.'

'But you are happy being female?'

'If I wasn't, I would have come in jeans and a Tee, probably have had this cut off.' I pull my hair which is now down to mid back round to the front.

She turns to Rebecca. 'Is she a happy child?'

'Very. I couldn't wish for a better.'

She looks at me as though I have offended and then she smiles. 'Very well Saskia. I see you are just sixteen. If you request it, I can prescribe oestrogen.'

179

'Yes please.'

'Sign this form. Mum would you also sign?' She has turned to Becca who has sat quietly. She signs.

The consultant hands me a prescription. 'Give that to your GP. Obey the instructions, keep to the dose.'

'What about surgery?'

'When you are eighteen, minimum.'

'Can I go on the list please?'

'I will put you on the list Saskia.'

'Thank you.'

I shake her hand.

We leave and I'm leaping for joy. We pick Jenn up and I fling my arms round her. 'I've got my prescription. Mum doesn't have to buy anymore on line.'

I always hated those interviews. It felt sometimes as though they wanted me to be a sex maniac, throwing myself at boys to prove I was really serious about thinking I was female. I wonder, do these specialist consultants actually really know what they are doing? Have they really got into our minds and understand the syndrome they are treating? I don't think so. I believe they are just pandering without real understanding. Perhaps no one, not in our shoes, can understand. They need to know, that F to Ms and M to Fs are no different to anyone else. Even hetero, cisgender people have different needs, some want sex, some don't. We are the same. It's not about sex.

Chapter 10.   Saskia's Tale

Now I was officially on oestrogen patches, my painful breasts developed quickly and I caught up with other girls my age. I felt much more real, buying bras that I was actually going to fill naturally and I bought some really pretty ones.

Jenn and I worked hard. Saturday was our day off. Well often we had hockey matches on a Saturday and if we didn't, then we would go to the Mall. Sundays we would always make a family day unless of course we went away for the weekend.

Gradually the days of pain and grief had faded. Life as a Jennings was full of love. Simon was the ideal father for two girls, teasing and daring us, encouraging us to do what might be considered boy things, a week's kite surfing course, another parapente (paragliding) that is, jumping off the side of a mountain, and cycling. He bought us both good road bikes and we go out and do up to fifty miles.

We therefore lead a busy life. I love to look nice, well groomed but I have also learned that I can still look feminine and do sports. Doing sports, particularly cycling, keeps me slim. I can also eat more and I love my food.

Jenn and I love the Mall, raking through rails of stuff looking for that item different enough from anything else to be interesting and individual.

We meet school friends and sometimes they bring boys or brothers, or we just hook up with people we know slightly. We are two pretty girls, so boys in particular and some of the girls too, want to be with us. We'll go for pizza when we're flush (with money) or perhaps a toasted teacake, our favourite at a favourite café. We girls all swap notes on clothes and where we get them, on boys and films and music, downloading to our phones and listening to each others and of course, we're into social media, checking to see who's communicating or who's wanting to chat.

We giggle and joke, pretty harmless, but sometimes we do leave clothes shops in a bit of a mess, with things hanging off their hangers or at least not put back very well with all the buttons done up. Amy laughs about that and says we are giving someone a job, which if we didn't maraud like locusts, there would be a lot less jobs for young people to do.

Christmas comes around and it's always a great time in our household. Jenn's cousins, now my cousins, Jerome (I don't know where they dug that up from) and Ginny and their parents come over. They are a bit older than us but quite fun and it's quite good to hear what two people who have just started Uni are doing and the problems they have. Every year, it's taking it in turns, we go there, down in Sussex or they come to us in Hertfordshire. We also have Jenn's Granny who is ever so old, but still has all her marbles and a very sharp tongue. She was born sixty years before us and has a completely different view of life. Like she can't understand, and this is what she said, 'How young people think they will ever afford a house while they are zooming around spending money all over the World, weekends in Prague, stag weeks in Las Vegas and hen weeks in Portugal as well as gap years.'

'Didn't you do that Granny?' I ask. Yes I call her granny because I have no blood relations, well none that bother with me.

'No we didn't. We didn't have the money. Anyway, flying was dear back then. We concentrated on the essentials of life. What do you think they are?'

'Eating?'

'Shelter, that means a house, a roof over the head, warmth, food, and not mass produced muck, not MacDonalds, I would close them all. Make do and mend. Learn to cook. Grow your own. That's what we were taught, that's what we had to do.'

'Times have changed Granny.'

'Not for the better. The nation is riding for a fall, the world is heading for disaster.'

'Let's talk about something more pleasant,' Mum says.

The prophet of doom is otherwise quite kind, slaps our bottoms and calls us cheeky girls and slips us a twenty-pound note. For our part we take her arms and make her dance with us and she does. Talk about dad dancing, she does a gran dance but when the music is to her taste she goes sort of wild and she's quite nimble for someone so old.

'Gran,' Jenn says, 'you are very old. Things have changed so much.'

'You are sixteen, just over a fifth of my age. In fourteen years time I shall be ninety, you will be thirty. Then you will be a third of my age. See you will be catching me up. So you better behave and make the best of everything. Don't waste time it's precious. Don't grieve for what's gone, it's over and won't come back. Look after today and look forward to tomorrow but don't wish your life away. Especially you Saskia, I know your operation is really important but enjoy the now.'

I blush. She just says whatever she wants whenever she thinks. I don't think she is frightened of anything. She was telling mum about walking down for her newspaper and there's a party of teenagers on the way back from a party. One boy has his enormous penis out and says to her, 'Bet you'd like some of this.'

Our eyes pop. 'Gran! What did you do?'

'I walked towards him and said, 'I'll rip it off you little fuck and stuff it down your throat.'

'Granny!'

'Mother!'

'Well what do you think I should have done, broken down in tears?'

'What happened Gran?'

'His mates told him to put it away and they went off up the street.'

'Mother! Did you report it?'

'I phoned the police. They thought it was funny. There you see. Proves my point, the World this country has gone to the dogs.'

'Gran we're not like that.'

'A good thing too. Just make sure you never are.'

I know we won't be.

Chapter 11.   Saskia's Tale

Easter holiday and we are not going away. We have exams in just over two months and we two are revising hard. When we are not revising we are on the bikes, peddling fast around the lesser used roads, trying to avoid the motorists that think all the room a bike needs is the width of the handle bars.

It's excellent doing the same subjects at the same time. We swap notes and test each other and download loads from the Net, a lot from the Beeb, British Broadcasting Company who do a lot more than just East Enders which we are banned from watching because mum and dad say it's so gross. When I get into the Beeb web site, I find there are all sorts there from sport to politics, world events and even pages of stuff on our exams and subjects too.

We work so well together, exercise together, relax together and laugh and cry. Jenn is really, the best. There's a boy across the road, Jason Grover, well a bit down from us who I think is really sweet on her, stuck. When we see him in the street he sometimes falls apart and blushes, it's so sweet.

I ask if she's going to give him a go, encourage him? Go out perhaps?

'I can't be bothered. Anyway, he's such a boy and too young, besides I'm busy and I have my sister to keep me company. I'll date in time, but not just for the sake of.'

'Yeah but don't you have to start somewhere, kiss a few frogs and find out things.'

'I like frogs, but I wouldn't kiss one Saskia, would you?' We giggle.

'Well I'm not ready. Anyway I don't know whether I'll ever. I think maybe I'm best on my own.'

She looks at me hard, like she does when she is trying to understand me. 'I hope you really meet the right person. Will it be a boy or a girl?'

'I don't know. I haven't a clue at the moment. Let me get rid of this; have my bottom surgery, then I'll see. He would have to be someone very special.'

'I hope you find that someone. Look when we go to Uni, we may be parted, not even at the same one. We must phone each other all the time.'

'Of course. Jenn, you're never going to lose me. I hope you'll always want me, but we will lead our own and well, different lives, like, you will probably marry, I probably won't. You I hope will have kids, so I can play with them and be a really silly loving aunty. We will be apart though.'

'Yes of course, but still close.'

I really hope so.

Summer term and the work is all revision. We are either at school, working or on our bikes. The exams come and go on for three weeks nearly.

A week later after Jenn and I return from school where we've been playing tennis, Mum hands me a letter. I know it's from dad immediately. I pull a knife from the drawer and slit the envelope. I read his carefully written letter, a nice hand but a letter that gives little information but in the simplest terms. What it says is, he's bringing his new family over in the summer and he would like to visit.

I sigh and close my eyes. I think I'm going to cry but I don't. I hand the letter to mum.

'What do you think Saskia? You don't have to see them. It's entirely up to you. Think about it. He's given an email so you can easily email back, you have time therefore to mull it over.'

'What do you think? My first thought was no, then I think, it might be right. To say no is a bit weak. I should face up to it and be proud.'

'Is that what you intend then, to see him, them, I presume he's bringing wife and his new son.'

'Tell me what you think.'

'You need to make this decision. I'll back you up whatever Saskia, you know that. I think you have decided haven't you? Well I think it's never good to have hatred in your heart. See them and close the door on what happened six years ago.'

'I'll email then, dates when we're here.'

'Use the planner here, our holidays are on there plus your days away with your friends and your cycle training.'

I email dates and I get an email back. They will be here for the third week in July, so that will not clash with things we're doing.

When we go to bed, Jenn says, 'You're quiet Sas. Are you OK.'

'Yeah I think so. It's a bit disturbing, having them come over.'

'Why not sleep with me tonight?'

'Yes I think I will Jenn. It will be like old times.'

We slept together for the next week until I felt on an even keel again. I still wondered what he wanted.

At last term ended. Unfortunately the rain began and we had a week of wet and cold windy days with westerly gales. We went to the Mall a lot and met friends and just hung out.

The next week and dad and family were in town for two days. It was arranged that we would eat at their hotel on Tuesday evening, the whole family so I would not be too exposed.

I dressed carefully, a Miss Selfridge blue bodycon with cage neck and cap sleeves. It showed off my figure and my slim smooth arms. Mum and Jenn did my hair between them. It was long and softly waved and shining.

We met them in the bar. Dad was much changed. He'd put on weight and grown a goatee beard. He had also lost some of the hair on his head, a receding hairline. Leaving everything from just in front of his ears intact but just a tuft on his forehead. I felt nothing for him.

He got up as we entered, recognising Simon and Rebecca and Jenn and I by association.

He kissed Rebecca and shook dad's hand. He turned to Jenn and kissed her cheek and then turning to me, he attempted to kiss me on the lips. I turned my head so he landed on my cheek. I think he noticed because he gave me a look. Well what did he expect from a sissy?

Of course my half-brother Michael was in bed. His mother had changed her hair. It now looked like a bad copy of Hilary Clinton's, although we soon found out that they were both rooting for Trump, the man they thought would get America moving. That was not endearing to me. I was already very political. Well I think if one is gay or trans one needs to be. Jacquie for that was her name, was much more attractive in real life than in her photo.

After all the introductions and we were comfortably sat with drinks on the table, Rebecca asked about hurricanes and twisters. Dad Simpson replied that most twisters occurred in the Mid West, East of the Rockies and west of the Adirondacks. Hurricanes came out of the Gulf and yes his rig was in the Hurricane area and so was their home.

He turned to me. 'I'm eternally sorry I treated you so bad. I just had no idea what you must have been going through. I read those websites and, well they explained a lot. Can't turn the clock back. You look good Saksia, look like your mom when she was young.'

'Her name's Saskia, John.' Jacquie said.

'That's what I said, Saksia.'

We all laughed.

'You've still got it wrong,' I say, 'Saskia, Sas-kia.'

192

'I'll try again, Sas-kia.'

'You've got it.' I say.

'And you're still clever?'

'Top of the form, well they are both.' Mum says.

'You look happy now Saskia.'

'That's evident and she should be. Two lookers in your family Rebecca.' Jacquie says.

'Yes and you might think they are actually sisters. They are always together. I don't think I've ever heard them argue.'

'Two girls and they never argue?'

'No we don't. We differ sometimes, well a lot, but nothing that really matters. Jenn just laughs at me when I get annoyed, but in a loving way.'

'Saskia had two or three bad years after, well you know. She would go into her shell and give us that look. But she was never bad natured. More hurt than anything.'

We went in to dinner. Jacquie kept popping off to see that Michael was OK. Dinner was fine. As Americans do, they ate with just a fork in their right hands. Dad Simpson seemed to have assimilated a great deal of America. There was a twang, a drawl to his voice and once even a y'all. I was quite surprised.

I was quiet. I didn't know what to say to him, so my answers to any question were monosyllabic.

It seemed a long time at the table, with Jacquie popping off between courses. At last we retired to the lounge for coffee.

Across the coffee table he said, 'You don't have much to say Saskia.'

'What should I have to say Father?'

'Well I am your dad.'

'No Simon is my dad. This is my family. I was never anything to you when we were a family, because I didn't conform to your ideal of a son. Well I never was a son. You were horrible to me and then you have reappeared on a nostalgia tour and expect me to fling my arms around you and shout 'Daddy'. It isn't Disneyland.' I was still in control but only just. 'The way you treated mum when Nick died...... I'm sorry, I need the loo.'

I went to the Ladies and found Jenn right behind me.

'Sorry Jenn. He makes me so wild, thinking he can just swan back into my life and all is forgiven. I suppose I should have flung my arms around him and shouted 'Daddy, my daddy!' I can't.' I burst into tears as the door opened and mum came in.

She took my hand and produced a hankie as mums always seem able to do.

'I'm sorry mum.'

'Well it probably needed saying.'

'He's not my dad. He never was a dad to me. It was always Nick. I'd come home with a super school report and he wouldn't even give me a well done. What's he want from me?'

'I think he is full of remorse. He knows he messed up.'

'Good. I hope he feels bad.'

'No you don't. Come on go to the loo, then repair your makeup and we'll go back.'

I did as mum said, reluctantly. If I'd not had the support of Jenn and Mum, I wouldn't have ever seen him again.

When I returned to the lounge, Jacquie was gone, presumably to see to Michael. At least she seemed to be a good and caring mother.

My father stood as we returned. 'I guess I had that coming. Just let me say something and then you can tear me to shreds if you like.

'Things between mum and I hadn't been good for some time. What happened to Nick and what was going on with you just opened up the whole can of worms that was our marriage. We hadn't made love for about four years by then. So Nick's death was the last straw, not you although I didn't understand you, I mean I didn't even know what was going on in your head. Still all that is no excuse. I should have been as good a dad to you as I was to Nick. I'm not an educated man, and I was brought up in a household where men were men, mainly manual workers. Nick was right in the mould, you were far from it. I know a lot different now, Jacquie is actually a very clever woman, a medical degree and a practising psychiatrist. She educated me and when I said I had you on my conscience, she said I had to come see you. I'm pleased I have.

'I look at you and I see a pretty young woman in a beautiful happy and loving family. Looks and brains. I'm sure you'll go far. I'd like very much to take you two girls out tomorrow, just us three. Do anything you like.'

Jenn looked at me. When I didn't reply immediately, she took my hand and looked into my face and nodded. I gave a small nod of assent.

'Father I don't know how I feel, but I'll try to be nice.'

'Then I'll pick you up around nine. I thought we could go to a theme park or something.'

'Not a theme park Father, it will be too frustrating, queuing all day. How about a day on the river, take the car to Putney and then get the boat to Emirates Air Line.'

'If that's what you'd like. We'll have a nice lunch somewhere. Wear something pretty and I'll be a proud man out with two gorgeous girls.'

'Still the male chauvinist Father.'

'What's that mean? Never understand that sort of talk. Men are men and girls are girls. Girls are pretty or should be, and you two are. I better get upstairs. Pick you up tomorrow then, nine sharp. Good night Rebecca, Simon, pretty girls. Till the morning.'

We watched as he disappeared in the direction of the lifts. Jenn giggled. I smiled.

'Actually in the end, I quite liked him. We'll see how we get on tomorrow.'

Chapter 12.   Saskia's Tale

Father turned up right on time next morning in a hire car, on his own. We were ready to go, excited about a trip on London's river. I just hoped the day would go well. I recognised that he was trying to make up and very different from the blunt man's man he had been.

An hour and a half later we arrived in Putney and caught the river bus. Dad had grown up in Hammersmith, so it was like a nostalgia trip for him. I realise I just used the word 'like', banned in our household as being as meaningless as 'you know' and 'um'. Some of our friends manage two or three likes in a sentence.

Simon says that we, Jenn and me, are intelligent and don't need to adopt the sillier mannerisms of our age. If we want to go to a good University they will not want students who say like unless it's I like work, sport, politics, debating, helping the sick. I think we get the point.

Anyway dad doesn't have to tell us about the river and the landmarks because it's all on these telephone things we hold to our ears and we pass under the various bridges including the foot bridge that crosses from St Pauls to Tate Modern. Father tells us that when it opened it rocked so much from people walking they had to close it for months and fit shock absorbers. He has booked a table for lunch at Tate

Modern because he has free tickets courtesy of the tour company he's travelling with.

We arrive at the Emirates Sky thingy and cross the river in the cable car which is quite thrilling, and then we get the river bus to Tate Modern. We walk in and see some of the exhibits and my father is contemptuous. A drill head would be a better exhibit he says than this junk, a load of stones laid on a floor, in one case and a fruit tree of condom leaves. Well at least that makes Jenn and I giggle.

We go up to the restaurant and we have a super view across the river to St Pauls Cathedral, probably the loveliest of all our cathedrals Rebecca told us before we left, as lovely and airy inside as out, built by Sir Christopher Wren against much opposition from all sorts of people at the time, ten years after the Great Fire of London. As we sit waiting, Father is reading from his guidebook.

'I'm learning more about London now than when I was a kid growing up here. One thing studying for Rig Captain taught me was, books aren't just hard work they're learning. I hope you girls know that.'

Jenny touches my knee beneath the table. She is smirking, well almost.

Dutifully I say, 'Yes . We both like reading. Girls read more than boys, that's a fact and did you know, girls read earlier on average too. Boys tend to be better at maths.'

'Is that a fact? You always were a clever girl. Do you play sport Jenny?'

'Tennis and hockey. We both play them. I used to swim but not now. I play cricket and we cycle.'

'And Saskia?'

'Tennis, hockey and I cycle, a lot, more than Jenn. We both do ballet.'

'Ballet?' He looks at me.

'Yes father, ballet. I like it. I'm way behind Jenn but it's good. I wish I'd started earlier.'

We ate our meal and looked across the river. There was hardly any activity on the water other than the buses and tour boats.

The lunch was fancy, very small portions and looking at the menu, very expensive. Afterwards we crossed the Millennium Bridge and went into St Pauls. It was as Rebecca had described but we didn't stay long. Father was uncomfortable there, whereas I could look at it just appreciating the beauty and engineering skill of building it three hundred and fifty years ago.

'That's one thing about the US and especially the southern States, a lot of religion. Jesus, do they like a fiery preacher. If you don't go to church, you don't get no friends.'

Jenn bumped my knee again. Dad was getting so Texas.

We crossed back and walked to the London eye, the big Ferris wheel that every city now seems to have. It was supposed to be temporary but is still a great London attraction with views particularly over Westminster. Dad could point out a few things and we gathered more from a tour guide who was talking to eight other people in our cabin.

From there we crossed Westminster Bridge and into the War Rooms, Father particularly wanted to see where Churchill lived during the War with Germany when so much of the capital was destroyed by bombing.

We caught the Underground back to Putney and then home, stopping for a burger on the way. It was banned food for us, so we wouldn't tell.

Back at home father came in for a cup of coffee, then it was time for him to say goodbye. They were off to Scotland tomorrow.

I went out to the car with him. 'Well Saskia, it's been good; good to know you are thriving. I gotta tell you, when you were a kid, I hadn't a clue and I was an ignorant stupid prick, oh I shouldn't say that sorry. You're looking good. Work hard, make me proud, and show me that all this tragedy has not been for nothing. I was horrible to you, ignorant, rude, and uncaring. I can only apologise. I'm pleased to see you happy, pretty, well mannered and very feminine. Promise you'll write, email and let me know how you're going. I'm proud of you. It's been worth crossing the Atlantic just to see you. I hope you can forgive.'

'Yes father. I'll keep in touch. It's been good to see you. I really hated you, but I don't any more. Be careful and look after your new family. I'll see you again one day I hope and I'll send photos.'

He kissed me, and hugged too tight. Then he was in the car and disappearing into the night as I stood waving. I sighed and went in.

The visit had raised all sorts of ghosts and I was quiet for days after. He had unsettled me but at least, the hate I had felt was diminished. I wondered whether I would ever see him again?

Well mum said, 'He's only in Texas, it's not another planet. Perhaps before Uni you could go over, take Jenny too.

If you're not having a gap, you could at least have a summer in Texas. There must be lot's to see. You both ride, go to a dude ranch or something and see more of your family, your step brother will be four or five by then.'

'That's a nice idea mum,' Jenn says, 'we'll see won't we Sas. See how things go with the emails. I have to say, he was a lot different.'

'As though he'd grown up,' I say.

Chapter 13.   Saskia's Tale

I did not see my father again. They flew back from Scotland. It had been good to see a man much changed with a broader outlook. Whether that was his position as a rig captain or the influence of a new wife and child or just that he had learned lessons from the past, I didn't know.

I discussed the visit and our day out with Jenny. She had been indifferent to my father when we were two separate families, now she said, 'Well he was very kind on our day out and he has tried to put matters right.'

I had to concur. He had been quite sweet, patient with us, fun at times and generous. I suspect he now made plenty of bucks though he'd always been on a good wage. I was pleased I'd seen him, glad to expurgate the ghost of those last horrible days after Nick died. However, the visit had brought back memories of that last day, his letter to mum kept in a box in the loft and of course, my last sight of mum, sitting on her bed and rocking, broken-hearted.

Luckily, the next week we were off to the gîte in Brittany and Jenny mum and I had last minute shopping to do, costumes and beach towels a gallon of sun oil and after sun and the groceries we liked to take.

On Friday we were on our way, the long trip down to Plymouth, ferry to Roscoff. It was always exciting, watching the coast of England recede and the sunset before we turned into our family four birth outside cabin.

We were so lucky with the weather that year. After the rain earlier in the month including a gale, we had sun and sun, dawn till dusk. It was never boiling hot, a breeze off the sea keeping us reasonably cool, but we had long lazy days on different beaches all around the coast.

After two all too short weeks we packed and were on the way home, our skins a nice uniform light tan and roses in our cheeks as mum said. Even our hairs had lightened in the sun.

Three weeks later and we are at school waiting for our envelopes with our results. We both open together in front of the head. We have glorious sets of A stars across the board. We embrace and dance round. We talk to our friends and listen to their successes and commiserate with those that did less well. The good thing is that all our friends will also be in the sixth form.

Mrs Simpkins the head says, 'Well girls, now you have another two years studying for A levels. They are even more important for those of you going on to University. I look forward to seeing you in two weeks.

In the sixth form we are allowed freedom of dress within reason, sensible not too sexy blouses in white or pink and grey skirts, heals no more than two and a half inches, shoes not embellished with adornments of any kind. We can wear ear studs but not drops. We can also uses minimal makeup, mascara but not liner, eyebrow pencil. No shadow or lipstick. It all sounds pretty straightforward but we know some will push the boundaries. Oh yes, we can use some colours of nail varnish, pearl, translucent pink or just plain.

We do things differently, using ring binders rather than exercise books and we use computers all the time. Now we are both specialising, taking four subjects. I am doing biology, chemistry, maths and English. Jenn is doing physics instead of English.

As sixth formers, we hook up with the boys' school for dances and drama; I suppose the idea is to break us into the world of sex gradually. Not that we seem to have much time for boys. We both play hockey for the school and Jenn also plays lacrosse. We still cycle, with a club doing time trials when we have the time. We still go to the Mall looking for bargains and meeting our friends. There's lots of homework. We seldom have three or four hours with nothing to do.

Simon, dad spends time with us, getting us out away from books, on our bikes and we go for longer and longer rides and weekends away in Derbyshire and Yorkshire, quieter roads and hills. Rebecca spends time making sure we grow up able to support ourselves, making us cook, simple and quick but nutritious and not fattening. We are lean; both size ten, a B cup. Jenn has more in the hip than me. I'm slightly envious.

The first year passes in a flash. I email Father once a month and I receive a short message back from him and more from Jacquie.

August and we are both working, me in a nursing home and Jenn in a laboratory to show Uni that we are heading in the right direction, it will be good to put on our CVs.

Most of the people in the home are women, seventy plus, some still very bright others not so, their minds and bodies breaking down. They mostly like to see a young female face and want to talk. I don't mind. The things they say can be quite shocking, even rude, but they mean no harm. It certainly keeps me on my toes. The home smells. It is not nice but I guess after a time one doesn't notice. Some are very sweet and hang on to my hand so tightly I think they are trying to get a transfusion of youth. It's quite distressing to think that they were once bright and young too. I guess that's life. It's a good lesson against the arrogance the young tend to have, thinking we have all the knowledge and savvy. The stories some of these old people told me were humbling.

I also do three days with my GP just sitting and listening to patients. Well that's what I want to do, be a doctor. I feel I would rather be a consultant than a GP. GPs have to know so much and use their powers of deduction given so few clues as to the nature of a patient's problem. Some seemed to come armed with as much knowledge as the doctor, others were almost incoherent in explaining their problem. Some were so obviously overweight yet they would not admit it and not admit that being obese contributed to their problems.

Into our last year and we are prefects but neither of us got head girl. That honour has gone to Mary Peters, whose talents also extend to music and drama. We don't mind. Better that Jenn and I are the same and that's what Mrs Simpkins the head tells us, she could not choose between us so thought it better to go to a third person.

Christmas looms in our final year and dad emails to come over to Texas, but I turn the offer down, making work loads the excuse and asking to defer until school finishes which will be for us the last week in June after our A level exams.

We have our interviews for Cambridge and keep our fingers crossed that we've done OK. I tell them I am trans and they ask about my future I say I will have surgery I hope in

August. That's when it's scheduled and I just hope the date doesn't slip.

They ask quite a lot of questions about that and about my old family. I manage to stay calm and truthful without getting embarrassed or flustered. I think it goes OK. Now I will have to wait and see whether they make me an offer. I was surprised that there were so many foreign students, French and German and an American as well as we English all going through the process. Cambridge is a Top Ten University so I guess it's to be expected. Medicine is really difficult to get into.

I cross my fingers and hope I've done well. As I sit waiting with mum for Jenn I think of my birth mum and I'm suddenly so sad that she can't be here to see me. I hope she would have been proud.

I still have these times of regret that my life could not have been more straightforward, but self-pity is self destructive and even regrets do one no good. Only the future matters. My life could not be improved upon. Becca and Simon are perfect parents and my sister, well we really love each other. We never tire of each other's company. We do sometimes disagree, but we shrug and say OK and move on. It's a brilliant relationship.

Christmas comes and goes. Back to school. Work and more work studying for these A levels and we have to get at least three A stars but four would be better.

Jenny has a boyfriend. She is not really keen, says she hasn't the time and anyway, there was an initial attraction but when they went out together, she found him quite boring. They kissed, she told me after, and it was like kissing a slavering bulldog. 'Ugh, enough to put me off for life. It won't but it taught me a lesson. Just because a boy's handsome, it doesn't mean he's desirable. Jeremy is defo yesterday.'

Those months we worked really hard, either revising or testing each other, doing specimen papers downloaded from the Internet or we would be on the bikes. I managed to win a time trial in my class, the first real solo sporting achievement. I'd come a long way from my sport hating days when I was in the Simpson family. I told Father in an email. Days later he emailed back, 'Well done'. The first praise he had ever given me.

In May Jenn and I hear that we have both been accepted for Downing College at Cambridge. It is one of the few colleges we didn't visit but I looked on the Net and it looks brill with a super reputation and its right next door to the Science Labs. The first hurdle has been jumped. Now we need not good but excellent A level results.

Exams at last. It's something of a relief that it will soon be over, for better for worse, we can now only do our best and hope we have studied and revised the right things.

The maths exams seem to go on forever, but at last we have completed everything. We compare notes, together and with others and it looks as though we have done OK. We are pretty well free agents but as prefects we are asked to appear at certain times, like lunches but it works out about twice a week.

My letter comes from hospital. My operation date clashes with going to Brittany. We have a family conference. I say they can go without me but they won't and perhaps I need their support. It is very important to me but to them it seems much more of an ordeal, a trial as though it's a grave situation, like cancer. For me it is deliverance from what went wrong in the womb. If I can't change my brain and sexuality, feeling of gender being a basic instinct one is born with, then I have had to change my body to match my girl brain. That's the simplicity of it. I don't think people who are not transsexual understand, but to us trans it is not much more than for a 'normal' person having a grotesque growth removed. Our bodies are so foreign to our minds, well in my case and others like me, that we would do anything to rid ourselves of the cruel joke nature has played.

I know post operative transsexuals complain that enjoyment of sex has been taken away, that's why some now elect to stay intact, but for me and others like me, my male genitalia is an important feature of my dysphoria and I cannot feel whole until it's gone.

I want to get this done before University, so I cannot delay and hope they give me another date.

Dad is great. He cancels everything although it cost's money. We will go to Brittany, the last two weeks in August. By that time I shall have had two weeks to recover and our exam results will be known. It is going to be a summer I shall never forget.

Chapter 14.   Saskia's Tale

I had all my pre-op tests done on a trip into London with mum and Jenn. After the tests we went to the theatre and saw Mama Mia. We thought it was better than the film, funnier and with people that could actually sing. My op is in five days time.

On the appointed day I attend hospital by seven am. It's always that time, regardless of where one lives or when they actually decide to operate. For those living far away, it means an overnight in London somewhere. In our case it meant dad driving us into London leaving home at five fifteen. They all came with me. I went into hospital, showing my chitty at reception. Dad sat in the car to avoid parking charges because parking round there in Fulham is really difficult.

We go up to the Ward and find reception. I wait and they say they are clearing a side ward for me. I wonder what happened to the last patient. Regardless, I'm soon installed in a barrier nursing room, that has one bed and it's own bathroom. I look out from five floors up on the Chiswick flyover, the road to the West. Mum and Jenn help me settle in, putting on the utterly unbecoming hospital gown.

After the op I can wear my own nightie. There's a last minute examination and when mum and Jenn are allowed in, they come with flowers. I am in bed and chatting when a nurse comes in with an injection. Mum and Jenn go and I'm alone feeling slightly out of it.

I am on my way, on my bed and the ride is surprisingly smooth and I find that mum and Jenn are in the lift. They give me last minute kisses and I enter the theatre suite, people in green and blue gowns, lots of masked faces looking at me, this is the scariest bit and I feel like dropping off the trolley and staggering away, a canula stings as it goes in to my wrist and I'm commanded to count and I get to five and nothing.

I shall not bore you nor shock you with what they do. The next thing I know is that I am back on the ward and a nurse is slapping my face quite gently and asking question like do I know where I am, what's my name, what's the colour of my hairbrush. They ask these questions just to see whether I am compos mentis, that surgery has not damaged my brain.

I'm not uncomfortable; I'm not in pain. The nursing sister says I have to ring if I need something and I have this drip in my arm and a pump giving pain relief. Mum and Jenn are still here apparently and they come in when the nurses have finished. I can remember smiling and they hold a hand each and there are kisses and then I fall asleep. When I awake it's dark and I'm alone. A nurse enters and asks if I'm all right. I say I am. She changes my bottle that captures my urine and replaces it. She hands me a glass of water and orders me to drink. I do. I must drink 250 millilitres an hour she says and points to the jug of water that has graduations down it.

I snuggle down. My middle is all bound up. I put on the radio and find some music and set it so I can just hear. I fall asleep. I'm woken again and made to drink or they say, I will get kidney failure. That I don't want.

Morning dawns and I hear the ward come to life, the squeal of trolley tyres on the nonslip surface, footsteps, distant voices, the clank of I presume metal on metal. A nurse appears and reads my temperature and pulse. She asks if I have any pain and I tell her I feel fine. She refills the water jug. Drinking all this water is really hard to do and has already become a chore.

I sleep again. When I awake, mum and Jenn are there. We kiss and chat and then it's lunch. It's no worse than school dinners and it's not what I asked for. I wonder who ate mine?

Mum and Jenn are back. They are going home and will be back tomorrow evening when dad will drive them in and then collect them.

I tell a nurse about my family. 'Dad's don't like visiting,' she says, 'men are so squeamish. They would rather not know that's why so many die with illnesses that could have been prevented. Such cowards over their health and bodies.'

That's the male race damned.

Fourth day. The catheter is removed and I can pee. I go in the bath and they say, if I feel like a pee then just let go. It works. The worst has been the removal of the drains. I could have killed the nurse, it was like having a red hot poker drawn through my new labia. The pain lasted only a few second with no pain afterwards. It's remarkable. No pain support and not even a dull ache or throb. I close my bathroom door and look at my anatomy in the mirror. I am hairless because that was removed prior to the op. There is some swelling, some bruising but surprisingly little damage to see. I look like a prepubescent girl and I'm thrilled that at last I appear as I have always wanted, always pictured myself. Thank goodness that thing has gone. Now I feel I can at last get on with my life.

Fifth day and the family collect me in mid afternoon after I have been prodded and examined and given a clean bill of health. I can use my oestrogen patches again. I have washed and dried my hair, made my face and dressed in a little grey mini skater dress that looks and feels like silk but is only polyester. I say goodbye to the nurses and mum carries my bag and Jenn and I hold hands. Mum phones and dad stops in the car park and we get in and are away. The big event is over. Now I have to learn to look after my new anatomy.

'You look a bit pale Saskia,' my mum says, 'do you feel OK?'

'I'm fine, a bit washed out but I'm fine.'

'Well take it easy. No dashing about.'

'No mum. I do have to shop though. I want to get a new costume for holiday and new knickers and with new knickers new bras and maybe some shorts or some culottes shorts I saw.'

'Yes dear, but don't think you are going to be back to your hundred mile an hour life style immediately, you are not.'

It turned out she was right. I was a lot more tired than I thought. I didn't do much for about a week, a few short walks, just to the local shops for emergency supplies, some panty pads and sweets and to the library for some books.

A level results day and we go to school to collect them. As we did with GCSEs, Jenn and I collect our envelopes and we open at the same time, extract the paper at the same time, eyes closed and one two three, we look. We both have four A stars. We are going to Cambridge, to Downing College, together still. It's so brill.

Jenn comes into my room when I'm just chilling out, lying on my bed on a hot august day, my window open and the curtains moving gently in the breeze. I'm reading a novel, 'All the Light I Cannot See'.

'What are you doing?'

'Just reading Jenn. Why?'

'I had a thought and I wondered….?'

'What?'

'You might tell me to get lost.'

'Come on Jenn, this isn't like you. What do you want to borrow?'

'Nothing, I just wondered if I could see, see what they did in hospital.'

'Is that all?'

'I thought it might be a big deal.'

'We are sisters aren't we?'

'Yes but, you've always had this thing about your body. I thought…I'm being curious, I shouldn't have asked.'

'Look we are going to be undressing together at some time and I've seen you, you saw me before, so better you see after.'

I lower my briefs and lie exposed.

'You look like, well a girl. What happens inside? Can I see or tell me to shut up and go away.'

'Of course you can see, silly.' I part my legs and show her.

'Oh gosh! How do they do that? You really are a girl.'

'But I can't have children.'

'Nor can some women Sas. Honest, Sas you are real, a real woman. You have no man left in you. You do feel that don't you?'

'I suppose I feel like any incomplete woman, a woman without a womb, a woman who cannot conceive. There will always be that little part missing and the experience that brings. I'm lucky that I transitioned at ten years old. Some have to wait until much older, even into their sixties.'

'Why?'

'I suppose loyalties, circumstances. It's happening for kids much earlier now, pre-puberty, so that's good, better for them. I met a lady in hospitable who transitioned at thirty-six. She regrets above all, not having her teenage years, her twenties and all the fun and excitement of dating and feeling her way as a young woman. At least I have had a female teenage and now I am as complete as I can be before I'm out of teen years, so I'm lucky.'

'And pretty and brainy. You have it all Saskia. We have it all.'

'Yes but have I the confidence to date.'

'Oh Sas, that's for you to decide. I think you should. Any boy would be lucky to have you.'

'Unless he wants children.'

'Surrogacy or adoption. It's not impossible.'

After two weeks I am feeling pretty well and on holiday in Brittany again. I have recovered my strength by the second week and Jenn makes me exercise with jogs along the beach, swims at low tide when it's safe and games of beach tennis and petanque.

Mum makes sure I eat well and have plenty of sleep. I'm at peace at last; my body as near to my ideal as I and surgery can make it.

I have the best family, intelligent, hardworking and loving. Eight years have passed since that dreadful spring before my eleventh birthday and I can't wait to get on with the rest of my life.

Chapter 15.   Saskia's Tale

We arrive back from France and immediately start packing for Uni. We have both elected to forego a gap. We have long courses, particularly me in medicine and it's really sensible to get on with it. We also think that 'the Gap' is a bit passé, old fashioned and self-indulgent. We have wonderful and generous parents and we do not have the right to expect them to finance us on a year long jolly.

Uni is costing enough. New laptops, sports equipment, almost a complete wardrobe for me, books and folders, phones and subscriptions for them, the latter the most expensive item. What on earth did we do before we had mobiles? Are they really necessary or good for us?

Finally the day comes and it takes mum's and dad's cars to transport the two of us the eighty miles. We travel in convoy and arrive in the college together where we are allowed to unload but there is no room to park. Mum and dad drive off to a car park and we find our way to our allotted rooms. We find we are in the same quadrangle but on different sides. We can wave at each other.

Mum and dad help us settle in. Afterwards we go for a meal that is a peculiar affair, we two are bubbling with excitement as well as anxiety and apprehension. Mum and dad are looking empty nest syndrome in the face. They are worried for us, out in the wide world on our own and hoping that the mores and standards they have taught us will serve us well. They don't read us a catechism of do's and don'ts. They have brought us up well to be charitable and kind, thoughtful and generous and to be hardworking.

By the time we finish eating it's dark. We walk to the car park and stand in that smelly and slightly evil place and wave goodbye. We promise to phone, often, after all mum says, that's partly why they have given us these super phones.

We two walk to our new home. We haven't investigated everything yet and over the next days we will. Tonight we are tired we kiss goodnight in the courtyard and go to our separate rooms. From here on, we both know our lives will diverge. We are now on different courses and different paths. We hope to be in the same social set but have sworn that whatever interests, boys, sport and work demands, we will stay close.

It's settling in that's difficult. Not into my room, not even the work and lectures, but socially. OK it should be easy. I look like a girl, act like a girl and sound like a girl, but within me is always a fear of discovery and from that the fear that I will not be accepted will be ostracized. I imagine in my dark times, the discovery of my origins flying around the campus and the nudges and sniggers and speculation about my body.

When after a month I still have these fears, although life has been good till now, I tell Jenn of my inner torment.

'I knew that's what was going on and I wanted you to tell me, have the confidence to confide. Why has it taken so long?'

'I don't know Jenny. I suppose I felt ashamed to admit even to my sister these doubts in my mind.'

'You've had a few offers from boys but you've always turned them down. Somehow we have never had this conversation, is it boys or girls?'

'You know I love girls, I love everything about them and I'm sceptical about boys, I mean the whole male race, their domination, aggression. That doesn't mean that individually I dislike them. I don't like Russia, but that doesn't mean I don't like all Russians.

'What do I know about boys? I've never really mixed with adult males of the species, except my dad and my Father. Your dad has been fine and I love him, but not like I love mum. It's so different what I feel for him. Jenn I feel totally mixed up. I'm bloody lost in the sex thing.'

'When I look at a boy, I sort of sort them automatically. It's either ugh or mmm. The mmm I can picture him, imagine being clinched, kissing. The ugh I imagine grimacing if he touched me. What do you feel?'

'Oh I do get that. Sometimes I see a boy and I think he's really nice, you know, his expression, how he behaves, just little things. I've seen boys with girls and sometimes they don't seem to care at all, the girl may as well be a backpack, an inanimate object he carries around. Other times, I see a couple and the boy is really interested and caring. Then I do feel pangs, I can think, I wouldn't mind some of that! Is that what I should feel?'

'It sounds like exactly how I feel. Firstly, you can't be attracted to every male of the species, life would be intolerable. Secondly, you have to remember what you would want out of a relationship. If all you want is a good rogering, there's plenty that will jump at the chance though you may find them disappointing. If you want a relationship, a meeting of minds, where you share ideas and ideals and likes and dislikes, that's a lot harder to find. I haven't found the right one yet. So you're not alone there. I just feel you're frightened, in case they discover who you were. You never were Edward were you? Those first ten years when you lived as Edward, you were acting, badly, as a boy. When you became Saskia, the real you emerged, this lovely whole person. You have to be more confident.'

'I know you're right Jenn. I have to have the confidence to go on a date.'

'Well as you know, I'm seeing James and I think he might be the one. Yes it's early days, but he's very stable, fun but not stupid, a brilliant scholar by all accounts and he plays rugger for the University, just a Half Blue but hopes to get a Full Blue this season. I really like him. His housemate is a lawyer, a studious type but fun. I've met him, Larry, a couple of times. He wants a date. I showed him a photo of you and me in France and he said, wow. I think he's a regular guy. Not that tall and not that keen on sport but he plays squash and rows and he cycles, and road trials. Will you double date? Blind date?'

'Wow! Throw me in at the deep end why don't you?'

'You have to try Saskia.'

'OK, perhaps I do.'

'You have the equipment now.'

'Yes but that's not what I had surgery for, it was to get rid of what I hated having.'

Jenn laughs and I don't mind. We giggle. 'Since we are being so intimate, have you?' I ask.

'No. I'm fending him off. I told him not to be impatient. I said I had to talk to mum first.'

'You didn't? What the hell did he say?'

'He went beetroot; I thought he was going to burst, and then he saw I was joking. He got the joke in the end. I told him I wanted it to be really special and now was not the time.'

'And? Was he OK with that?'

'Yes. I see it as a bit of a test for him, see how committed he is. If he waves goodbye over it, then I know he wasn't the one. I'll be upset but not heartbroken.'

'Jenn I so admire you.'

'Good! So what about you and Larry?'

'Larry who?'

'Your date, the Honourable Lawrence Murberry.'

'Honourable? You know what I think of titles.'

'Don't be an inverted snob. He can't help being born with that.'

'Who is he? Is he really nice.'

'I think you'll like him. His father is in electronics of some sort.'

'Do you like him?'

'He's different. Yeah he's OK. You're different and don't be upset. You are. You can be devastatingly direct. You pull no punches. Please, just go out once. If you don't like him or men or whatever, you don't go again.'

'OK then. When is this big event going to be?'

'Friday. Just a Pizza and a glass or two. Larry is loaded, so it won't cost you a bean.'

'Jenn you're so mercenary.'

'Mm no, just I believe in letting those pay who can. All these rich people have got rich by taking money out of their workers pockets. I don't mean that entrepreneurs and company bosses shouldn't be well paid, but they are handing themselves millions while their workers are on minimum. Nothing against Larry, he didn't make the rules. If a boy can pay, then let him as long as he doesn't think he's buying me. In any case, we know that all through our female lives we will be paid at a lower rate. So you are up for it?'

'I'll probably be sick, but yes.'

'Six thirty Friday. I'll see you before then.'

Chapter 16.   Saskia's Tale

I checked myself in the mirror yet again. This was not vanity, it was making sure that no Edward was showing. Yes I know you will say I'm silly Ed was years ago. I can't help having these self doubts even after all these years. Jenn would be mad with me, but I'm haunted by my past. Actually, I look OK, I know I do and everyone tells me I do but I haven't that confidence.

I remember seeing a documentary on some famous model, everyone said she was beautiful, but she too had self doubt. Even more excuse for me then. I just feel that if I can look beautiful, then there will be less doubt about me, people will not look and say, obviously a trannie. They won't. I am, thanks to the T blockers, feminine. As Jenn says, you look like a girl, you sound like a girl and you have girl bits, therefore you are a girl.

So tonight is the night, when I go on my first date with Larry. The Honourable Lawrence. I'm wondering what I've let myself in for. I asked Jenn what he looked like, not that it matters, and it's his character that counts after all. Nicer if he looks also OK.

There's a knock on my door and I twirl from the mirror, switch off the light in my windowless bathroom and cross my bedsit accommodation to the door. I flip the lock and Jenn enters.

'Good job,' Jenn said. "You'll knock him dead.'

'I just want to look good. I haven't dressed to impress.'

'No? Who are you fooling? OK, but you will.'

I collect my bag and we exit, locking my door behind us. James is waiting in the entrance. James is huge, his shock of dark blond hair as unruly as normal. We walk through the Mall and across the Market and down Trinity Street, past St John's and across the river. We enter the pasta and pizza restaurant.

We thread our way to the table. The young man with his back to us also rises. He's six inches shorter than James. He turns, the chair scraping on the floor as he does so. He grins and holds out a hand and grasps Jenn's hand and hisses her on both cheeks. It is then my turn, the same ritual kiss. He has a little stubble, more than James, and I experience a slight thrill as we are cheek to cheek.

We sit opposite the boys. Larry is not unhandsome. He has a slight twist to his bony jaw and I think a superior sardonic air. He is also studying me. He's a dark haired young man with very brown eyes, about five nine. I try to remember who he reminds me of and I have it, Tom Hughes, the actor who I've just seen in Victoria. He's lovely.

He sits easily. We study menus and order. We have a bottle of Aussie Pinot Grigio, lightly scented, a hint of sweetness. Larry fills our glasses and orders another bottle.

We chatter about our courses. Larry is doing his masters in Law.

'So what is going to be your law speciality? I don't really know anything about law except there are solicitors and barristers.' I say.

'Well I'm aiming at being a barrister specialising in criminal law. At the moment, it seems the most exciting and dramatic thing to do, though not the most rewarding. And what are you doing, besides looking really delectable.'

I look disdainful.

'Mm a bit sexist for Saskia, Larry.'

'I was just stating a truth.' He looks me straight in the eye. 'You've taken a lot of trouble with your appearance and then you don't appreciate a compliment.' He still smiles.

'I wasn't sure you meant it.' I say defensively.

'I don't really go in for flattery. I don't usually go on blind dates, but I was assured that you were brainy and beautiful. You are a beautiful girl. Very kissable. I know, it's much too early for us, but someone will be lucky one day. Are you a brain box? How broad minded are you?'

'I don't know. Why?'

'I have a joke. A man sees an advert in the paper for a proof-reader. He rings the number and says, 'You want a proof reader.' 'Proof reader?' the man the other end of the line says, 'no it should read 'Poof leader', it's for a gay scout troop.'

I laugh. No offence to gays but it is just funny and the sort of thing I hear newspaper compositors delight in doing, the deliberate mistake. What makes the joke more is the actual job offered is so bizarre compared to that advertised.

'You're funny.'

'I try to be. So you can laugh. Good, I wondered.'

'Hey Larry, go easy on her.'

'No, I think she's lovely. Saskia, I wish you would relax. You are not on the menu but I wish you were.'

And I do laugh. I have to. We all then chatter about things we like, films we've seen or haven't. Places we've been and then art. Favourite places, 'The Musée d'Orsay, in Paris lots of Impressionism, marvellous.' Larry says

'I've not been but I've heard of it.'

'Everyone rushes to the Louvre and while that is wonderful the Orsay is more. It used to be a railway station but you wouldn't know now. We could go. There's an artist Felix Valleton and one of his paintings on display was Interieur. A woman standing in her nightie. It took my fancy, so I looked him up. He died in 1925. He was years ahead of his time. I found this painting, 'Woman with a Cat', just brilliant.'

'So is there a point to your story?'

'Oh yes, the point is, one goes to the Orsay and one expects to see, Manet and Monet, Van Gogh and Henri de Toulouse-Lautrec, Seurat, Cezanne and the rest and then I find a new name and I investigate and I'm amazed, the man was so prolific. Always have an open mind. So dig down and you may even like me.'

'Is that what your whole story was about? Me liking you? Does it really matter whether I do or don't like you?'

'It matters quite a lot. Don't you want it to?'

'Well I want people to like me so I suppose, yes.'

'This is a bit intense Larry,' Jenn says. 'James is he always like this?'

'Not as bad. You are being quite annoying Larry old bean.'

'Trying too hard to make an impression on this girl. I'll shut up.'

'Well Lawrence, this is my first blind date too. I was warned you were different. I didn't realise how much of an egotist you would be.'

'Ouch, she has claws.'

'Anyway,' Jenn says trying to move the conversation to safer ground, 'James is getting his Blue on Saturday, so are we all going, the three of us?'

'I am,' I say.

'Of course,' Larry says.

'Oh have I to put up with you again?' I smile as I speak.

'You make me sound like a recurring boil. If you prefer I'll sit elsewhere.'

'No don't. I rather like sparring with you.'

'I've heard a lot about you from Jenn and I was interested to meet you, for two reasons.

'Really? I must be fascinating.'

'Yes you are, I mean I want to ask questions but now is not the time.'

We chatted, all four of us. We ordered and ate our meal and we strolled home via The Backs, the meadows beside the Rivers Cam. Jenn and James lag behind and kiss. When I spin around I see them.

'Would you say they're an 'item'?' Larry asks.

'Well I think they are fast on the way to becoming one. Jenn is brilliant. If James catches her, he'll be a very lucky man.'

'Are you with someone?'

'Oh no. No I really think romance and I don't mix.'

'What because you're trans?

My first instinct is to run, to leave him and lock myself in my room and listen to loud music but I can't.

'Yes I'm trans.'

'Why does that mean you should avoid romance?'

'I don't want to discuss this.'

'Oh, OK.'

We walk on in silence towards Silver Street where we need to cross the road. He takes my hand, felt for it and grasped it, not an elbow or upper arm, my hand.

'Saskia. A lovely name. Saskia. They're kissing again. Can't we?'

'Of course we can.'

And we do. It's really nice. I mean no tongues, just a kiss on the lips, a long and lingering one, his arms about my back and I actually put my arms about his body. He presses against my breasts, painful still from the oestrogen I take. I feel the hardness of his penis against my abdomen. We walk home hand in hand. He kisses my cheek occasionally.

He looks at me, his head slightly tilted, looking rather down his nose, his mischievous, I was going to say sardonic, smile. His dark eyes sparkle in the lamp light.

'I think you are rather a treasure. Fascinating. So I'll make sure we have good seats for the three of us at the rugby. I'll come to Downing and pick you both up, say half eleven, and we can go for a bun and a coffee or what you will, then to the match. You won't change your minds?'

'No of course not.'

'Are you with someone?'

'Oh no. No I really think romance and I don't mix.'

'What because you're trans? I am right.'

My first instinct is to run, to leave him and lock myself in my room and listen to loud music but I can't.

'Back to that again. Yes I'm trans.'

'Why does that mean you should avoid romance?'

'I already said, I don't want to discuss this.'

'But I think we should, if I'm to see you again.'

'See me again?'

'Yes.'

'Why does it matter to you if I'm trans?'

'Because it matters to you.'

'Oh you bloody sneaky lawyer.'

'I think we should get this in the open because it seems to be a block between us. I'd like to know you better. Another thing is, I am writing my thesis for my doctorate on Transgender and Transsexual People versus the Law. You could help me.'

'I see. Is that all you want from me? Well I'm prepared to tell you all I know if that will help you, with no personal emotional involvement. Have you been in love Larry?'

'No, not in love. In immature lust, a crush or two. And you?'

'Oh no not I. I'm not sure whether I will ever find someone or want to.'

'That's quite sad. I hope to find someone. You don't?'

'I have to be a realist.'

'Because your trans? Well there can't be another reason as far as I can see.'

My face burns even in the cold night air. We pass below a street light on the pathway that cuts the corner to Silver Street Bridge.

'Don't be embarrassed. Saskia, you should be proud of who you are. I think you underestimate yourself.'

'How did you know?'

'Ah you think I can tell? I can't. You are just a gorgeous girl. James told me and of course Jenn told him. They knew I needed help with my thesis. It doesn't matter to me. I like you. Here, let's cross.'

'Come on.' We trot through the traffic, giggling and look back at the lovers still the other side of the road. We stand on Silver Street Bridge and look over. There were still people sitting out by the river drinking.

We wait on the Bridge for the lovers to catch up. The river is black and oily. Light from the pub catches in it here and there where there's a ripple. A few hardy smoking beer drinkers still sit or stand out on the small terrace.

Jenn and James are still waiting to cross.

'They are still kissing. Can't we?' Larry asks.

He has taken my hand and holds it behind my back. He has moved close. The breeze ruffles his forelock. My back is now against the bridge parapet. My hair spreads across my face as a breath of wind touches us. I brush it away and back. My heart beats and I have a moment of panic and I want to run away. I clench my teeth and gulp and I think I'm going to burst into tears.

'Look Saskia. If I hadn't been told, I would not have known. James knew I needed first hand knowledge for my thesis, that's why he told me. I would not have ever guessed. You are beautiful and bright, intelligent. I really like you. Don't put up the shutters just because of this mean trick nature has played.'

He kisses me on the lips.

'Thank you. Neither of us will be so shy next time.'

'Next time?'

'Oh yes. I still haven't asked you the questions for my thesis. We had more important matters to sort out didn't we?'

'Did we?'

'Yes, your attitude to boys. Have we sort of established that I'm not a mass murderer.'

'I........I don't know about boys or men. Yes OK I've been frightened to find out.'

'So have we some understanding of each other?'

'I think we have begun to have.'

'You should be more confident, a pretty girl like you.'

'Lot's of people wouldn't think I'm a pretty girl.'

'I'm not lot's of people then. The lots you know must have bad specs. When I say you are beautiful I mean it. Look I really want to see you again. First thing is for my thesis which is Transgender and the Law but also, well I like you. So when are you free?'

'I'm pretty busy at the moment, an essay to get in as well as anatomy.'

'So you are studying one hundred per cent of the time. You haven't a few minutes to help out a poor boy with his thesis?'

'As like a business arrangement? I give you information, anecdotes and you what, buy me a meal? Strictly business?'

'Whatever, anyway you want it to be. I'll get the best of both worlds won't I? I'll be doing my research and I'll be out with a pretty and fascinating girl.'

'You Larry are a flatterer. So what do you suggest? Pizza just across the road, in Regent Street I think we have every kind of Eastern cuisine.'

'What food do you like?'

'Is there a budget?

'No, well as long as it's not a three star Michelin, well even one star.'

'So for picking my brains we're going to Spud-U-Like?'

'Are you always difficult?'

'I'm teasing you Larry. Perhaps if you buy the food, I should cook for you?

'No I want to take you out. Be seen with a beautiful woman. That's a very nice offer but no. OK I like Thai, do you?'

'I do and I'd love to come. Thank you Larry.'

James and Jenn have caught up at last.

'I'm picking you up to go to the match on Saturday.'

'That will be very nice Larry thank you,' Jenn says quickly, I think to prevent any prevarication from me.

'Shall we wander home, walk you back to Downing,' James says. 'It's a nice evening if a little cold.'

When we finally arrive at the ornate black iron gates of College, the boys leave us when we are safely inside.

Jenn comes to mine for coffee as I'm nearest the gate.

'So how did it go?'

'I like him,' I say.

'You do?'

'Very intelligent, knowledgeable. A typical public school boy and up himself, but he is clever and I think he's actually kind.'

'But you were so harsh.'

'I was. He just came over a bit superior and smooth. It's been a nice evening.'

Next evening we join the boys and go for a coffee. It's cold, as we walk home, not a frost, but a clear sky after a warm autumn day and there's a nip in the air. I'm glad of my coat. Again Jenn and James lag behind.

'Ah l'amour.' Larry says. I look at him sideways.

'You are so feminine. Your every action, the way you speak. Are you really sure you were born a boy? I would really like to kiss you again. May I Saskia?'

He kisses me gently before I can refuse. Jenn and James have still not crossed Pembroke Street what are they waiting for? I wish they'd hurry and I suspect some plot by Jenn to leave me alone again with this man. He kisses me again on the lips a gentle tingling tantalising caress kiss and something explodes within and blood seems to rush around my veins. He kisses again harder and his tongue plays with my lips. He still holds my right hand my left has lifted to his back. He backs me into this porch. His other hand is under my coat, his fingers in my waistband where the crack of my bottom begins. I look up at him and close my eyes and lift one foot behind me, instinctively. I'm aware and I think, why have I done that, why do girls do that when they kiss a man?

He stops and pulls away and gazes at me. 'There, not so frightening was it?'

I'm panting so hard I can't answer. I don't attempt to break away. I feel his warmth and enjoy his breath upon me. I lay my head on his chest. He has his nose in my hair and I hope the perfume from my expensive shampoo has not worn off.

'So dear Saskia, we are OK now? Friends? I haven't upset you. You needed kissing.'

My memory takes me flying into 'Gone with the Wind', Rhett Butler saying the same to Scarlett O'Hara.

'Oh fiddle de dee Rhett.' I say with a laugh in my voice.

'What?'

'I was just replying to your line, the one you stole from 'Gone with the Wind', you needed kissing.'

'Oh was it? I've never seen the film. I liked kissing you though. I've wanted to do that since we first met.'

'But we did the other night. I liked it too. You were right, Jenn apologised for you while we were in the loo. She thought you had been too intense, too full on.'

'I said you had gone to talk about me.'

'As you so rightly said, we talked about you, but not much. I said I liked you. Surprised?'

'Why would I be surprised? Everyone likes me.'

'Larry the modest.'

'A lot of what I say is tongue in cheek.'

'Ah then we have something in common. A lot of what I say is play acting.'

'Good, I'm glad. I won't have to try so hard then if you really like me. Well, young lovers,' Jenn and James have finally reached us, 'you've caught up at last. We were waiting so long, this young lady, Saskia, was forced to drag me into the porchway and kiss me just to keep warm. I liked it, so I allowed her to kiss me twice.'

'My sister Saskia is very choosey. You should think yourself very fortunate.'

We walk home my right hand in his right, his left inside my coat and blouse, his hand on my lower back. I'm excited and very frightened.

Chapter 17.   Saskia's Tale

We wait by the Porters lodge for Larry to collect us and he's late. 'Why didn't he just say he would meet as at a café?' Jenn says in annoyance. A thin drizzle has just begun.

'Inside,' I say, 'the nice Porters won't mind.'

We go in the Porters Lodge. 'Hello, we are being picked up, may we wait in here?'

'That's all right young ladies. Saskia isn't it. Lovely name, can't forget you with a name like that. So where are you off to?'

'Lunch and then the rugby.'

'Oh yes. Well I hope you'll be in the dry there. This rain is supposed to get harder as the day goes on. Ah here's a car, is this your ride?'

We turn and look out. A Mercedes SLK has come to a stop and Larry is getting out.

'This is us. Thank you.'

We leave the Porter's Lodge and descend the steps. Larry is holding the door open and we cram in quickly to escape what has become more than drizzle.

'Sorry I'm late. What a day! Father giving me some earache about choosing law but not commercial law.'

He turns the car and we head south out of the City.

'Where are you taking us Larry? Jenn I think we're being kidnapped.'

'Yes an Arab prince needs two new wives. I'll get a good price. Little place I know. All booked for twelve and seats reserved at the match. So no panic.'

We drive over the Gog Magog Hills. We wind round the outskirts of Fulbourn. The pub is busy and he parks with difficulty while we wait in the porch. He arrives and kisses us both. 'Let's get lunch.'

We have a nice lunch; plaice goujons and hand cut chips. We all drink shandy.

'Where do your parents live?' I ask naively.

'We have a house in Norfolk and another in London as well as Paris and a little place in Tuscany that we hardly use.'

'Oh my word. That's a bit greedy isn't it?'

'Um, well one might say so. On the other hand, we employ a lot of people, and the properties we own are not the sort of properties owned by people on average incomes. So we are not depriving the needy. We pay taxes. I would hate that you disapproved. Life isn't fair, Saskia. It never was.'

I say nothing more. I think about my attitudes to wealth. I'm quite silent as we drive to the match. Jenn makes up for me by chattering away. As we enter the stand he looks at me and holds his hand out. I put my hand in his.

'I'm sorry.' I say quietly.

'For what?'

'For being unthinking, about people owning property.'

'Oh. Have you changed your mind?'

'Yes. Well, it's still a lot of property but I guess your family pays for it. Our family own a gîte in France, so what's the difference except scale.'

'I'm going to Norfolk next weekend. Come with me and see the cottage. OK yes separate rooms, your own bathroom. I dare you.'

'Can I think about it?'

'Till the end of the match.'

'OK. Fine.'

'What you'd agree to that?'

'Well I think it's fair. You made an offer, I need to reply.'

'You're a lovely girl. I'd wait till the last minute if I had to.'

'Then the answer's yes, Lawrence.'

'Really? Good girl. Thank you. You won't be sorry. Oh and I shan't tell them you are trans. I don't think it's necessary so don't be nervous and defensive.'

'I don't think I will be. Will your parents be there?'

'Yes. Of course, and my older brother and my sister who happens to be your age.'

'And I'm just a friend. Will they find that odd or do you often take girls home?'

'Oh you think me a Lothario, dallying with damsels. I've taken a few girls home over the years and parents being parents, always think, this will be the one.'

'What if they hate me?'

'They will not hate you. They'll be bewitched by you.'

'Larry, this is a big thing for me.'

'I know. I nearly didn't ask because well, one I thought it might be too soon and two, I thought you might refuse. I feared being turned down. It will be fine. My parents are really lovely, just dad wants me to go into the company and criminal law is not what will be useful. I'll pick you up Friday, around three. Will that fit with you?'

'I have an essay to get in but yes, Friday by the Porters Lodge at three. Don't be late.'

'Of course not.'

We watch the match and it's exciting. James comes on as a sub so gets his full Blue. Brilliant.

The week passes quickly as it does when one is truly busy. I complete my essay and hand it in.

Friday I lunch with Jenn. I'm already a bag of nerves and I tell her so.

'You will be fine. Not too much makeup. You are inclined to overdo it, trying to hide the non-existent boy. Just remember, you are Saskia, there is no boy. No one can see any boy.'

'I know. I just hope nothing goes wrong.'

'What can silly? So Larry. Is he the one?'

'Jenn you are such a tease. I like him but it's far too early.'

'Darling Saskia. I tease because I love you. Well at least you are not so frightened of boys that you won't go out with one. Have a good weekend and tell me every detail when you come back. Larry's OK then is he? I thought you got off to a bad start.'

'We are both provocative. I think we understand each other now. Time will tell sister mine.'

'Are you taking some condoms?'

'Sister? Really.'

'It's not just about not getting pregnant, it's disease prevention as well.'

'I think it's far to early for that.'

'OK. Just thought you would want to find out if everything works. Here just in case, keep this in your bag.'

She hands me the condom in its blue and silver packing. 'Go on. Be prepared and I want a blow by blow account.' She giggles again. "You get the joke?'

'I was ignoring your coarseness.'

I take the small packet and put it in my bag. I have no intention of having sex, making love with this boy.

Friday and he picks me up on the dot I thrust my overnight bag and makeup in the back and sit beside him. We thread through the traffic and head north. We skirt Norwich and still head northwards until we reach rolling hills. He turns right and then left down lanes that seem impossibly narrow before turning the car through a brick gateway. We drive and an enormous Georgian house with a Palladian frontage supported on four columns two each side of an enormous door comes into view.

'Here we are at the cottage.'

'Crikey Moses. Well, I do declare Lawrence darlin' it takes me right back to the old plantation.' I say. 'Oh Larry, I'm really scared. Your parents might hate me, think me a pleb. This is so posh.'

'They are going to love you.'

Chapter 18.   Saskia's Tale

He carries our bags and we enter the massive black front door with the polished brass fittings and arrive in a circular hall with stair climbing like a vine around the side to the second story, and then onward to the third floor. I'm sort of awe struck, gaping when a door opens and a woman of fifty or so stands there.

'So here you are Lawrence. And this is the girl helping with your thesis?'

'Yes mother, this is Saskia Jennings. She's studying medicine at Downing.'

'Saskia, that's an interesting name. Were your parents Dutch or Slavs?'

'No they were English.'

'Oh but Saskia, such an unusual name. Well I look forward to getting to know you. Lawrence I have put Saskia in the blue room. Would you take her up? Dinner will be in an hour, time for a bath if you wish. We don't dress.'

'Thank you.'

'When you descend we will be in the drawing room dear.'

'Come on Saskia. I'll show you the way.'

We ascend and turn along a corridor that is covered with deep velvety red carpet. Our feet make no sound on the deep pile.

He opens a door. 'This is the blue room, fourth one on the left. You have your own en suite.'

I enter the room and he places my bag on the bed. I place my makeup case on the dressing table. Larry lingers.

'Right then. I'm across the way. Run in any time if you want something.' He takes me in his arms and kisses my forehead. I feel weak and suddenly really sad. Why? 'You're OK?'

'Yes Larry. I think I have everything.'

'Then I'll see you downstairs.'

He closed the door behind him and I unpacked my small case and laid out my toiletries.

I had a quick shower and changed into a cream dress that ended four inches above my knee. I wore crystal and synthetic pearl adorned wedge mules on my feet. I redid my makeup.

I descended the stairs and down in the hall found four doors leading off. I tried the door Larry's mother had emerged from. It was in darkness except for a table lamp on a sideboard. The table was laid for six.

I tried another door and found another unlit room, a library or study.

The third door I was lucky. I entered and found the whole family there a fire in the grate and curtains drawn. The TV news was on volume turned right down. Larry stood up as I closed the door behind me.

'Let me introduce Saskia. My father, my sister Julia and my brother Francis. Saskia is at Downing reading medicine.' I tried to take in the faces and smile sweetly. I shook hands with them all; I didn't know whether that was the right thing to do. I felt really gauche, out of my class.

I was found a seat beside Larry with Julia on the other side on the three-seater settee.

'Well Saskia, so medicine? That's a long haul. Do you have any idea what discipline you'll follow?'

'Well my instinct is paediatrician, but so many girls want to do that. I do want to work for MSF before taking up a permanent post. I shall just have to wait and see where my talents lie I think.'

'So how did you two meet? Larry tells us nothing.'

'My sister, also at Downing is seeing James who is Larry's house mate.'

'So do you go out in a four often?'

'Mother! Stop fishing. Saskia is not my girl friend, she is my friend who happens to be a girl and has gracefully agreed to assist me with some of the medical and psychiatric aspects of my thesis.'

'So how does one become an expert so young?'

'It's a subject that fascinated me and I've done a lot of research on trans children. That's why I want to be a paediatrician.'

'Still specialising in that field?'

'Well maybe. It's an area that is very underfunded because the numbers of children now coming out as trans is increasing exponentially.'

'Exponentially?'

'Oh sorry, for example, if the number coming forward with the syndrome this year is one hundred and next year one hundred and fifteen, the year after might be one hundred and thirty five. The clinics are overwhelmed.'

'Why is it increasing so much?'

'The theory is that now the syndrome is out in the open and more accepted, instead of going with conditioning or the expectations of how a child of either sex is supposed to be, children are saying honestly, they don't feel like their birth sex.'

'So we are bringing misfits into the world because they have a whim?'

'Oh no, not a whim. Not misfits, no I don't like that description. Mostly they are very ordinary, often intelligent largely law abiding. No imagine, if you Lord Murberry, were born a boy but your brain tells you to be a girl. It is not an easy path, not a whim, it's a compulsion. They have brains that are the opposite of their birth gender. They are literally trapped in the wrong body.'

'But how?' His mother persists.

'It happens in the womb. Brain and genitalia develop at different stages, a matter of just a few weeks but if the mother has a hormone imbalance during that time, there can be a dichotomy between brain and genitalia.'

'Well I can see why Lawrence is consulting you. You obviously know your subject.'

'There's just one other point I would like to make. Some physicians like to point to the statistics from the USA of attempted suicide by fifty per cent of transsexuals. It is not the same here. In the USA, there is much more antagonism to transsexuals engendered particularly by religion and of course, a redneck, backwoods agenda. For example, North Carolina and other states brought in the Bathroom Bill that says people must use the bathroom of their birth gender. You can imagine what pain that causes a trans person and how dangerous that can be. These red necks, sometimes educated red necks say the law is to protect women. Women are not in danger from trans people. It's trans people that are in danger from cisgender people.'

'What's cisgender?'

'Oh yes, cisgender people for example born female or male and behave as their genitalia would suggest they should. They have done mental tests on transgender people and cisgender people. Questions requiring an instant response or choice. The cisgender people respond as you would expect a male or female to do. The transgender people respond the opposite of their birth sex. Psychologically, they are the opposite of their bodily gender.'

'Wow Saskia, you do know your subject.' Julia says. 'Mum was hoping Larry was bringing home a girl friend, but you really are an expert helping him aren't you?'

'I suppose I am.'

'And you would specialise in that?' His father asks.

'Perhaps. It's very underfunded, so there are not many posts. The two main clinics are in London. There are six thousand and counting on the waiting list for a first appointment. The best outcomes are if children change gender before puberty. They can delay puberty with hormone blockers with the idea that by the age of sixteen, they will have the maturity to decide on their future. Stop the hormone blockers and natural puberty clicks in.'

'Well I think it's very disappointing. I thought Larry had found a girl at last.'

I looked at Larry. He was still cool. 'Oh I like her a lot. We have kissed but we are not what you would call going steady. Saskia is very single minded, very industrious and serious about her course, determined to get a first. I respect that.'

'Wow bro, you've matured.' Francis said. 'I thought you were the Casanova of Old Cambridge Town.'

'Oh. I hadn't heard that.' I say.

'I used to be young and foolish.' Larry says.

There's the ring of a gong. 'Well, dinner is ready.'

We all rise and make our way to the dining room. I'm feeling quite confused.

Chapter 19.   Saskia's Tale

'How was your weekend?' Jenn asked.

'OK. Jenn they live in a mansion, ten bedrooms and four reception rooms.'

'Oh, you didn't have to share a bed then?'

'No Jen. He didn't make any suggestions and I was I suppose quite thankful. They hinted that he'd had a lot of girl friends.'

'Umm, I guessed that from what James said. He is four years older. So when are you seeing him again?'

'We haven't made a date. No plans.'

'Oh that's disappointing. So you still haven't tried out the equipment?'

'No Jenn.'

'You need to sometime.'

'Have you with Jamie, that great ox of a boy? He'd squash you.'

'No. I don't think I can hold off much longer.'

'You can't hold off or you can't hold him off?

'I can't hold off.'

'Oh so it's serious then?'

'It's serious enough to want to find out what it's all about and whether, you know, I like it with him or for that matter, whether I like it at all.'

'You haven't doubts about that?'

'No I like boys but one wonders. You must wonder too.'

'Oh for me it's more than for you. I'm sure you will be fine. This is the first time I've ever seen you worried about anything Jenn. My whole life is postulated that as I wanted to be female then it must be boys. I wonder. I have to find out, but I don't think it will be Larry.'

'No? That's a pity. I hoped.'

'I liked him, he likes me. I don't think he can get his head round the trans thing, even though I have helped with his thesis and we have kissed and cuddled. He made no move on me over the weekend. I wondered whether he would want to commute in the night, but no.'

'Well if not him, there will be someone else.'

End of term. Dad came and fetched us. Jenn said bye to James who had come to the College specially to give her a Christmas present.

Christmas break was the usual, a family Christmas and work while we're at home.

I was surprised on Christmas morning to have a phone call. My phone started ambling across the marble worktop as I was helping in the kitchen. I wiped my hands and picked it up. 'Hello.' I recognised his voice immediately.

'Happy Christmas Saskia.'

'Happy Christmas Larry. Where are you?'

'On top of a French mountain. It's snow as far as you can see. I was thinking of you.'

'That's nice.'

'What are you doing?'

'Cooking Christmas dinner.'

'Oh, for the family? How many of you?'

'Just us four.'

'Oh nice. Look I'm sorry I didn't see you after the weekend at my home. Things were a bit busy and I had to use all the material you gave me.'

"I understand. We are on two different planets Larry.'

'Oh is that what you think. It's not as wide a gulf as that is it?'

'I'm me and you are you, different schooling, different up bringing, different class Honourable Lawrence. Besides, who am I?'

'You are a beautiful girl that's all that matters. I think of you all the time.'

'Really? I find that hard to believe.'

'Why else would I have let the family ski off without me, while I sit here and ring you. I'd like to se you when we get back to Cambridge.'

'Well you know where I live Larry.'

'Yes.'

There's a long silence. I stand watching while mum and Jenn fill mince pies and put their hats on. I wonder if he is still there.

'Look Saskia, I really like you. I want to see you again.'

'I'll be at Downing, same room. Give me a call. Look I must go, things to do Larry. Be careful on those skis.'

'Snowboard. Yes I'll be careful. Saskia, have the best Christmas. I'll see you in Cambridge.'

'Larry, have a good one. Give my regards to your family.'

'I will. They liked you.'

'Of course, everyone likes me. Bye Larry. Thanks for phoning.'

I switched my phone off.

'Right mum. What shall I do now?'

'Brussels Saskia would you please.'

'Was that Larry?' Jenn asks.

'Mmm.'

'And?'

'I don't know.'

The End.

Dear Reader,

If you like this story, ***<u>please</u> leave a review of this book***. Go to the page on Amazon and scroll down to Reviews. Click on the box, 'Customer Reviews' and write a few words. You can choose whatever review name you like for yourself, so it is anonymous. The only condition is, you have to have purchased the book. Thank you.

Best wishes for a happy life, Adrienne Nash.

PS. I too am trans and every day is a happy day. I escaped my boy body after some years, back in the mists of medical science when even doctors had no understanding. If you are trans and you are sure, be brave and have a good life.

28891443R00158

Printed in Great Britain
by Amazon